DIRTBAGS

*For
the Bone*

DIRTBAGS

a novel

TERESA McWHIRTER

ANVIL PRESS | VANCOUVER

Copyright © 2007 by Teresa McWhirter

Anvil Press Publishers Inc.
P.O. Box 3008, Main Post Office
Vancouver, B.C. V6B 3X5 CANADA
www.anvilpress.com

All rights reserved. No part of this book may be reproduced by any means without the prior written permission of the publisher, with the exception of brief passages in reviews. Any request for photocopying or other reprographic copying of any part of this book must be directed in writing to access: The Canadian Copyright Licensing Agency, One Yonge Street, Suite 800, Toronto, Ontario, Canada, M5E 1E5.

LIBRARY AND ARCHIVES CANADA CATALOGUING IN PUBLICATION

McWhirter, Teresa, 1971-
    Dirtbags / Teresa McWhirter.

ISBN 978-1-895636-88-8

    I. Title.

PS8575.W484D57 2007   C813'.6   C2007-906042-0

Printed and bound in Canada
Cover design: Mutasis Creative
Interior design: HeimatHouse

Represented in Canada by the Literary Press Group
Distributed by the University of Toronto Press

The publisher gratefully acknowledges the financial assistance of the Canada Council for the Arts, the Book Publishing Industry Development Program (BPIDP), and the Province of British Columbia through the B.C. Arts Council and the Book Publishing Tax Credit.

PART ONE:

Circling the Block

1

Vancouver is a place that can kill people with loneliness. Cold, grey rocks break up the beaches. It is a city full of powders. A city filled with rain.

Spider's mother was the best-looking of four ugly sisters. She'd insisted Spider stay with her Aunt Clara in North Vancouver when she arrived in the city. At first Spider missed the sound of the small town she'd left, how the mountains were so quiet a person could hear right to the middle of them. But that was nothing like the lights, the traffic, the people crammed on every block. The noise slammed all the way down to her bones.

Spider spent her first few weeks in the city wandering downtown. When it rained no one bothered her as she walked the quiet, wet streets. She was a dark-haired girl with sad, delicate features and gold-brown eyes. The damp weather hurt the old break in her arm. She tried to blend into the city crowds, and sometimes took random bus rides across the bridges into downtown, sitting in the back just to look at people.

Aunt Clara painted terrible watercolours of horses during the day and watched soap operas like it was her job. She was a stick-thin woman on a disability cheque. Sometimes she worked cleaning houses. Clara's apartment was small and everything smelled like cigarette smoke, even leftovers. She liked to recount her health problems—asthma, kidney and gall stones, bursitis, arthritis, and chronic fatigue syndrome—to anyone who'd listen. Spider noticed Clara coughed loudly into the phone. For someone with lung problems she had no trouble sucking down a few packs a day.

When Clara was feeling well she went to the track. At night she played bingo, or quarter slots at the casino. It pleased Spider that someone in her family could surprise her. Becoming a gambling addict was the most interesting thing her aunt had ever done. Clara had a lucky change purse, key chain, and a dried chicken wing. The guys knew her name in every pawnshop in town.

One night out of sheer boredom Spider went to bingo with Clara. She walked around the smoke-filled hall but the only person her age was a boy with scabs on his shaved head who kept turning to twitch in her direction. Spider sat with Clara and Clara's neighbour Gerda. Gerda was a small, wrinkled Swede who wore puffy hats, and was always getting into car accidents. Her neck brace lay on the seat beside her.

"I was telling Gerda that you're looking for a place to live," Clara said. "She has a daughter about your age—"

"My daughter is crazy," Gerda said.

"She's a very nice girl," Clara argued.

"Nice yes," Gerda said, dabbing her cards in a frenzy, "but last week she dyed her hair pink. Pink! I said, 'What are you doing? You look like a clown!'"

"What's her name?"

"Agnes." Spider had a mental image of an obese girl in an apron who enjoyed scrubbing large pots.

Her aunt said, "Why don't you call right now?" Spider wondered if Clara wanted to get rid of her. She'd even dug out a quarter.

Spider went to the phone booths at the back of the bingo parlour and dialed. A girl picked up on the first ring. "Hello?"

"Hello? Agnes?"

"Who's this?" There was instant suspicion in her voice.

"My name is Spider Mackenzie. I got your number from

Gerda. She said you had a place to live. I mean, you need someone to live there."

"Call me Blue," she said. Her voice meant business. "Don't ever call me Agnes."

"Okay."

"I fucken hate that name."

"Sorry." There was an uproar in the bingo hall as they called the winning number of the meat draw.

"So....*whaddya* want?"

"Gerda said you had an extra room."

"Hold on." Blue muffled the phone for a minute and came back. "Well, you'd kind of have to see the place," she said. "My roommate Sally is fucked for money and the landlord hates us. If we're late with the rent he tries to evict us. What's your name again?"

"It's Spider."

"Right. Spider. It's a really small room. Do you have a lot of stuff?"

"Almost nothing."

"You got a job?"

"Not right now, but I've got rent money. I just got to town."

"From where?"

"Some little place you've never heard of," Spider said. The metal cord twisted and she wanted to hang up the phone then pictured the black duffel bag full of weed under the bed in Clara's laundry room where she slept. *I really have to move that,* she thought. She told Blue, "I've got some money tied up in…investments right now."

"Investments?" Blue laughed like she read her mind. "So, you know my *mom*?"

"Uh…from the bingo parlour."

"Oh Christ," Blue laughed. "Okay. Come by tomorrow and we'll check you out."

dirtbags > 9

Blue gave her directions to an apartment on the eastside. It was an old wooden building with crooked front steps. There was a park across the street. The houses in the neighbourhood on the other side of the park looked even worse.

Spider buzzed number six and a tiny woman with short, dark hair and pink streaks came down the stairs. She wore faded jeans and a red bandana tied across her head. There was a silver hoop in her nose.

"I'm Blue," she said and opened the door. "You're Spider?"

"Yeah. Hi."

"You cool?"

"Sure," Spider said. "I just took the *cool* bus here."

Blue eyed her up and down suspiciously. "Those are some big apple catchers."

Spider looked down at her too-big overalls. "I wish I could say it was laundry day," she said. "But I practically live in these." Actually, her mother had threatened to burn them. She shrugged and said, "I guess I just like to dress like a plumber."

"It's good not to flash too much in this neighbourhood. If no one knows what you've got they won't rob you!"

"Are you serious?"

"This is kind of a shitty part of town," Blue admitted. "Everyone here's *vaguely* criminal, but it's nothing you have to really worry about."

"I'm cool," Spider said, but was pretty sure she wasn't.

"All right," Blue said. "The apartment's on the second floor."

The lobby had high ceilings and iron radiators. It smelled like cat pee, spices, and Friday night parties long past. Loud music blasted from the top of the stairwell. They walked up one flight of stairs.

Spider liked the apartment right away. It had a long hallway with hardwood floors and a red ceiling. Someone had painted the bathroom a shocking electric blue. There stood an old clawfooted tub beneath a tiny, perfect window. "That right there is Sally's fart chamber," Blue said. "The bedroom next to it is mine. And this would be yours," she said. "Ta-dah!"

The room was the size of a walk-in closet and would barely fit a bed and dresser. Spider eyed the room impassively. The first two words in her head were "tiny" and "shit-box."

"It's a closet."

"No it's not," Blue said. "Look, there's a window!"

Sure enough, there was a small window that looked down into the alley. Spider could barely fit her head out of it. "Hmmph," she said. It didn't seem to phase Blue at all.

"Hey, you want a beer?"

"Sure," Spider said. The kitchen was small and clean and opened into the living room, which was quite large. There was a couch covered in a Mexican blanket, and a big coffee table with deep burns in the wood. A couple of comfy chairs and a TV, a huge coloured rug under it all. Heavy blue drapes covered the windows, and a few gig posters hung on the walls.

Blue rummaged through the fridge. "Tara was staying here until this guy upstairs said she could house-sit for him while he was away so she split and fucked me and Sally for rent. Right when Sally got fired like a total jackass!" Blue handed her a beer and they cracked their cans. "God, Tara was such a pig. She left hairballs in the bathroom as big as rats!"

"So, you guys need someone right away?"

"Uh-huh. And it's only two-fifty a month!"

They drank a second beer. Blue told Spider that her father was from England and some kind of scientist who followed migrating birds. He had made great advances in the study of the bluewinged Heron. "I'm *not* bragging," Blue assured her. Gerda had run away to Paris from Stockholm to model when she was sixteen.

Her parents had moved a lot and Blue had never been in one school for long until they stopped in a prairie town where her father had abandoned them. Gerda wasn't the same after that so Blue had left town when she was sixteen and started to travel. She'd ended up in Vancouver at the age of twenty-three.

"This is a nice place," Spider said, looking around the apartment. It was better than living in Clara's laundry room. "I'm staying with my aunt but I sense it's time to go."

"It's cool with me if you move in right away," Blue said. It was a week until the end of the month. "But Sally has to give the okay. Oh, check this out." She opened a giant cupboard underneath a ledge in the living room. "This is all yours," she said, and peered inside. "Christ! Half of Tara's crap is still in it." There was a heap of dirty laundry, condom wrappers, balled-up socks, a few scattered tampons, and a stack of porn magazines. "Oh, the life of an Internet hooker," she sighed.

They walked down the street and Spider bought a six-pack of beer. Back in the apartment she and Blue cleaned out filthy Tara's cupboard together.

Sally walked into the apartment with another six-pack. Sally Pepper was a tall, strong-looking girl with short dirty-blonde hair and a crooked, sweet smile. "Look Blue," she hollered, "don't get mad, but Rodrigo wouldn't lend me any fucken MONEY. OKAY!"

"Sally...relax," Blue said. "This is Spider. She's thinking about moving in. She knows *Gerda*."

"Really?" Sally asked, plopping down on the couch beside Spider and cracking a beer. Her face and arms were covered in freckles. "Where did you meet Gerda?"

"Uh, at bingo," Spider said.

"HAH!" Sally laughed. It was a friendly sound and Spider liked her right away.

"Just so you know, Sally's a chronic pothead," Blue said. "And she hates cigarettes!"

"I don't *hate* them," Sally said. "I just don't understand why people would smoke something that didn't get them high."

"How long have you lived here?" Spider asked. "It's such a great place."

"A year," Sally said. "I moved out, and Tara moved into my room. Then I came back and kicked Tara into the..." Sally paused here, "little room. I missed this place," she said, looking around. "The only good thing about Oscar dying is that I came back."

"Sally's cat was like her baby," Blue explained.

"Yeah," Sally agreed. She took a big swallow of beer and got up to look out the window. "Hey," she called down. "What's going on in ten-dollar-blowjob alley tonight?"

"Sally lived in a house with a bunch of hippies," Blue said. "Because there was a big yard for Oscar."

Sally put her head back in the window. "That was the only reason I was there and what did those stinking hippies do? They left the GATE OPEN!"

"Right onto the highway," Blue said.

Sally choked up. "He was just like her baby," Blue said again. Sally pulled on a ball cap low. She looked like a tough mechanic.

Spider said, "What's orange and looks good on a hippie? Fire."

"HAH HAH!" Sally was a really cute girl. When she laughed her mouth fell right open.

"I *hate* hippies," Blue said. "Remember that hippie boy from Rossland? He gave me scabies!"

"Those were flea bites," Sally said. "From his dog."

dirtbags > 13

"Whatever," Blue said.

Sally shuddered then brightened. "Hey, Blue, that reminds me. Did you know that someone set a car on fire last night, just down the street." Blue just shrugged. "I love this neighbourhood!"

Sally lit a joint and they all cracked another beer. Blue smoked a cigarette and told stories about her job. She waited tables in the same place where Sally had been fired for coming to work drunk.

"I'm the world's most successful waitress," Blue said. "If people don't tip I chase them down the street and tell them, 'If I wanted to work for minimum wage, I'd sit in a lotto booth!'"

Spider pulled out some weed and rolled another joint. "You know what's fun?" Sally nudged her. "Getting Blue stoned."

"I never smoke unless I'm totally wasted," Blue said.

"And then you say ridiculous things."

"At least I didn't tell a census taker that drinking was my full-time job!"

The buzzer rang and Blue rushed for the door. "It's Glen with the beer!"

Glen was an aging beach stoner who sold homemade beer and used any occasion to strip off his clothing. Sally informed Spider he wore flip-flops all year, even in winter. They paid him for the keg.

"I'm having a party," he said. "Come by my place later tonight. Or any night!"

They had thirty-two pints of beer to drink between them, just over ten beers each. Sally calculated it should only take them two and a half hours, maybe three with bathroom breaks. A few pints into it the subject naturally turned to boys.

After Blue's father left, Gerda had run through a steady string of near-husbands, including a newly released convict she'd met in Vegas. Blue had her own special brand of bad luck. She had caught her first boyfriend cheating with another girl at her sixteenth birthday party. Then she'd fallen in love with a bad drunk named Jake in a small island city. A few years later she'd lived with an easy-going biker and come home to find another woman in bed with him while his kids played downstairs. After that Blue had sworn she'd never let her heart get broken again. She said her gypsy blood kept her unsettled.

"Do you have a boyfriend, Spider?"

"No." She said nothing else.

Sally patted her hand. "Too many dirtbags?"

Spider took a long drink of her beer. "I had a nice boyfriend, once. After we broke up I slept with his brother. Then I went out with this guy who dumped me for his ex-girlfriend when she came back to town," she said. "Then for a while he dated us both and I hung around for scraps."

"That's fucking horrible!"

A dark look came over Spider's face. "Last Christmas my brother Johnny was...well, he died in an accident."

"Oh, Spider." Sally reached over and squeezed her shoulder. Spider twisted away.

"When I called Andy and tried to tell him, he was with his new girlfriend and just wanted me off the phone."

Blue slammed her fist on the table. "That dirty little fucker!"

"I'm so sorry about your brother," Sally said. "What happened?" Spider inhaled on her cigarette and blew the smoke out sharply between her front teeth. It sounded like a hiss. She didn't answer. Sally and Blue arched their eyebrows at each other. It didn't go by Spider unnoticed.

"How did—" Blue began. Spider interrupted her.

"I don't really want to talk about it," she said. There was a awkward silence. Spider cleared her throat. "Do *you* have a boyfriend, Sally?"

"No way," Sally said. "I wouldn't waste my time on any of those fools!"

Spider laughed and then caught Blue looking at her. Something on her face made her smile seem jagged.

Spider thought, *That's how I look, too.*

When the keg was empty they decided the beer hadn't gotten them drunk enough. Blue slammed her tiny fist down on the table. "I wanna go to that fucken party and get our money back!" Sally Pepper agreed.

They stumbled to the party but couldn't find Glen, so they stood in his kitchen and helped themselves to shots. Sally lunged at the joint being passed around. It went out when it got to Spider and she wondered at her ability to re-light it. Blue saw Glen first.

"That was shit beer!" she slurred. "We want our money back!" He snickered and the sound of it made Spider furious. She lowered her head and made a drunken run right into Glen's soft gut.

Glen went "AH-GUH" and slumped against the counter. Blue and Sally laughed so hard they couldn't stand up straight. Spider got pushed out the door and someone kicked her in the ass. "Leave her alone," Blue bellowed. "Today's her birthday!" Blue was a small girl but took up a lot of space. Spider yelled and smashed a flowerpot.

Someone said, "Who *are* those chicks?"

"EAT MY SHIT!" Blue screamed. They walked down the block swearing and came back to rip up all the plants in the yard, then ran chortling down the street.

Spider woke up on the couch the next morning. Someone had wrapped a blanket around her and taken off her shoes.

"Mornin' Scrappy-Doo," Blue said from the kitchen. She wore child-sized pajamas decorated with cowboys and held a cigarette between her fingers. Her short hair stuck up in a back tuft.

"You're in," Sally said. She brought Spider a mug of coffee. "As soon as you gave Glen that head butt, I knew it was going to work out."

"That's great," Spider said, and propped herself up in the corner of the couch. "It'd be a good morning if I didn't feel like shit."

Outside a wedding party drove past honking. Blue ran to the window. "I GIVE IT SIX MONTHS!" she hollered.

"She always does that," Sally said.

"You know why people get married?" Blue said. "They turn thirty and think, 'I've got to get a lockdown on this shit before I get ugly!'"

Blue was a beautiful girl. Dark eyes and dark skin, arched eyebrows and high cheekbones, these features were so perfect they would make the things Blue did, like riding a skateboard while wearing an enormous fur hat, even more astonishing.

"We're going to the CC Saloon tonight," Blue said to Spider. "You in?"

"Sure," Spider agreed. She hadn't laughed that much in a long time. Sally and Blue were loud girls who took all her attention and energy. "I'll go get my stuff and come back later. Is it okay to walk around this neighbourhood late at night alone?"

Blue just shrugged. "I'm going to give you some tips on city living," she said. "When I walk into a room, the first thing I do is take note of the exits." She pointed ahead, then behind her. Spider's gold-brown eyes followed along. "Be smart. Look around. Know where you're going. Watch your friend's back and make sure they're watching yours. If you do that you'll be okay." Blue's eyes had power like the force of an impact.

dirtbags > 17

"I'll bet you can always tell when someone's lying," Spider said. When Blue laughed she sounded surprised, like Spider had managed to impress her.

2

The black duffel bag lay open on the living room floor. "I decided I could trust you guys," Spider said. "Well, as much as you can ever really trust anyone."

"Aw," Blue said. "That's so sweet."

"It's almost a pound," Spider said. "I need to start selling it."

"You're really bringing something to this friendship," Sally said.

"Can you fucking believe it?" Blue said. "I'd buy weed from this girl."

"She's got an honest face," Sally considered.

Blue asked, "Where'd you get it?"

Spider thought of Billy Newton, the look on his face when she'd got out of his car, the dagger tattooed on his neck. She said, "It's a one-time deal. From an old friend."

"Can you help her sell it, Sally?"

"Yeah," Spider said. "I'll give you a cut."

"How much?" Sally asked, and Spider saw then how there was a side to her that was strictly commerce and it was understood between them.

"How does a quarter from every ounce sound?"

"It'll keep you in weed," Blue told Sally.

Sally opened a baggie and smelled. "Deal." They shook hands

and she laughed. "HAH HAH HAH!" There was a lot of Sally in that sound.

"All right, ladies," Blue said and clapped her hands. "It's just about beer o'clock!"

Sally had on long baggy shorts and found a clean undershirt. Blue wore a short red skirt and a top that showed her tattoos. They looked tough. Spider put on more and more mascara in the bathroom.

"It's gonna be fun tonight," Blue said, wrapping silver chains around her wrist. "Just remember, men fuck who they *can*. Women fuck who they *want*."

Sally and Blue's favourite place to drink was the patio at the CC Saloon. Travelers stayed upstairs in the hostel and the kitchen served terrible food all day. The CC Saloon was a sprawling bar of open wooden tables with long benches. There were skaters and rocker chicks and old drunks and bikers and punks with dyed mohawks, all at some level of impairment.

Spider followed Sally and Blue to a crowded table and squeezed in at the end. They ordered a pitcher from the drunk-looking waitress. Sally said, "Last Saturday night this blind guy popped out his fake eyeballs right at our table!"

"They had little suction cups on the end," Blue said.

The bar seemed full of career drunks and party girls. "A lot of bar stars," Spider said.

"We refer to that specimen as glory whores," Blue corrected.

When they finished the pitcher, Spider followed Sally out the back door to smoke weed in the alley while Blue ordered another. They ended up in the back of a VW van and hot-boxed while Sally negotiated with the mullet-haired driver and sold him an ounce of pot for two hundred dollars. In the bar Spider ordered shots.

"High-roller," the bartender said, taking the money. "You got ID?"

She handed over her license. In the picture she was sixteen and smiling, straight brown hair and no make-up. Spider remembered that day. Johnny had waited at the DMV while she'd taken her driving test, and after she'd passed he took her to Mister Burger for ice cream. The bartender looked at the license then back to her blackened eyes and ragged hair. "Wow, your parents must be real proud."

"They're dead," Spider snapped. "Got any more funny comments?" The lie was worth the bartender's look of shame.

Back at the table they downed the tray of tequila shots. Spider was starting to feel very drunk and belched twice. The boy sitting next to her squeezed her knee under the table. "Everything here goes down in the bathroom," he slurred. "But the real deals are made out in the open."

Two punk-looking girls talked loudly at the next table. "I'm horny. I'm gonna go home and get friendly with my shower nozzle."

"Whatever you do, don't palm it and think of your ex. Don't give him that power."

"I knew it wasn't going to work out. He was stingy with the cheese!"

"Did you like him at ALL?"

"Well, I liked him better than TV."

"I think I'm attracted to men who are failures."

"But aren't they all?"

Spider sat enjoying their conversation when a heavy blonde girl pushed in next to her. The blonde's elbow smacked the side of her jaw. Pain shot down Spider's neck. For a moment her eyes watered and she blinked hard. The boy beside her leaned far away.

"WAAATCH it!" Sally yelled.

"Fahk off," the girl said in a heavy Australian accent.
"HEY!"
"Who's thit," the girl sneered at Spider. "Your girlfrind?" Sally suddenly reached across the table, grabbed the girl's neck with one hand and punched her face with the other. Once, twice and the girl made a wet, snorting sound. A bouncer rushed over.

"You're outta here!" he told the Australian, wrestling her from the bench. Her top lip was cut and bleeding. Everyone at the surrounding tables whooped and clapped. Sally pulled Spider with her to the bathroom where she covered her face with her hands. Spider saw that she was trembling.

"Oh my god," Sally said. "People were CHEERING." She began to sob. It surprised the hell out of Spider.

3

The Eastside. Chinatown. Blood Alley. Rat Beach. Lounges, bars, and strip clubs. Shelters and needle parks. Massage parlours, Korean BBQ. Bathhouses, casinos, skate parks, pool halls. Skid row and the train station. The bus depot. The docks.

The bright yellow noise of the city poured into Spider's room. She especially liked the sound of rain hitting the street and traffic in the morning. The light and speed and sounds of Vancouver kept the darkness in her thoughts from pressing down.

Sally Pepper was a stoner with a strong work ethic. She clipped pot plants, sold chocolate mushrooms, and took any odd jobs she could scrounge. In desperate times she'd baby-sat and worked telemarketing. Once she'd let a practicing masseuse give her a nude massage for eighty dollars. When he'd tried to put his fingers between her ass cheeks she'd rolled over and kicked him in the jaw.

It was the end of the month and Sally made phone calls. It was how she worked. Sally knew the codes that could crack the city wide open. Spider wondered if she didn't enjoy the hustle most of all. There were mushrooms to be picked up, ground into chocolates, then resold. Cheques to cash, weed to sell, debts to be collected and cleared. Sally had a phone number for anything—after-hour liquor or contraband bus passes or where to get Spider a cheap BMX. She was proof that getting enough money so you didn't have to work was the toughest job around. Everyone had some kind of hustle; trafficking stolen bike parts had become the new currency. Trying to live on a welfare cheque was an impossible joke.

"My father was an inventor," Sally told Spider. He had created the robotic Pet Pal, a Book Buddy for holding papers, and a device for separating yogurt curds. "When we were growing up we were poor then rich then poor again. I've seen it all," she said. "Money is an illusion. It doesn't mean a thing."

"I've already accepted being poor," Spider said.

"What was your family like?"

Spider stiffened. "My mother and father struggled pretty hard," she said. Thinking about her parents and the arguments they'd had over money was the last thing she wanted to do.

That night she dreamed of Johnny living on a beach with a girl in a white bikini. He ate fresh fish and seafood off the boats everyday. Spider felt so happy when she woke up. For a moment.

Spider enjoyed the constant commotion of living with Sally and Blue. They were hard drinkers and the phone never stopped ringing. People stopped by with bottles of wine or to get them high; they brought over their visiting cousins and skate videos and bags of shake that got cooked into hash oil. Friday and Saturday were booze marathons: cocktails at home, a night at the bar, a six-pack to take home. They watched the sky at six a.m. with an ashtray and the start of their hangovers, which could only be cured by specific types of greasy food. Sunday was strictly devoted to recovery.

Every Monday night Blue and Sally had a tradition to get ripped in defiance of the workweek at a place called the Quarry. Their friend Mandy was a DJ who also worked the door, a loud punk chick with huge tits and flaming girls on surf boards tattooed up her arms. She had a raspy laugh that rumbled out of her, and could kick any guy's ass in the place. The Quarry was a shitty bar with good drink specials and a hooker problem in the bathroom.

Spider made her bed everyday. She washed the dishes. There was a routine. On Sundays they painted their toenails. They went to cheap matinees in the afternoons when it rained. Once a week they gathered the empty bottles and took them back to the liquor store for more.

4

Sally got a job washing dishes in the kitchen of an expensive Greek restaurant, mostly because they didn't check her references. It was a four-star kitchen run by an alcoholic chef and she could take home as much food as she wanted.

One month had gone by in Spider's new home and rent was due again. Sally had been selling the pot in eighths and quarters. By then Spider had gotten to know a few of the customers. There was a doll-faced hairdresser who traveled in a clique of adoring drag queens and would drop anything for a hair emergency. She cut Spider's ragged hair into sleek layers. Also there was a graffiti artist who rode trains all over the country and sometimes slept in the basement; a Danish playboy who had named his baby after his last drug dealer; and Angelica, a beautiful Italian girl who lived in a townhouse with her five equally beautiful sisters, each one crazier than the last.

Spider's favourite customer was Crispy Jones. He got the name Crispy because he was always baked. He knew Sally Pepper from the neighbourhood and stopped by every day or so to buy a few grams of weed.

Crispy was a weird cat. His emotional response to everything was to stick his head out the window and yell. He also admitted he enjoyed lighting fires. Crispy had spiked blonde hair that stuck out when he took off his red ball cap. Sally's own nickname for him was Pot-Kid. He wore skate shoes to bed and bathroom slippers when he couldn't ride. Sometimes he went on crazy drug binges and made weird sculptures out of wire. Whenever Spider delivered to his place she found him doing things like drinking a glass of brandy in a silk jacket, or smoking a Cuban cigar on the roof in the middle of the day. Often they hit the bong and went exploring—the train yard, the alleys in Chinatown, Crab Park. Crispy was genuinely odd and sweet. House cats adored him.

He told them his girlfriend didn't like it when he got high, though he was such a weed head he usually smoked his whole bag and had to buy more before he left.

"Why are you dating a girl who doesn't like that you smoke pot?" Sally asked.

"I guess because girls make me spend all my time trying to figure out what I'm going to do the rest of the time," he said, scratching his head. He lit an enormous joint. "What's Tara doing these days?"

"Who knows," Sally answered.

"Have you seen her lately?" he asked. "Does she have a boyfriend?"

Spider had only met Tara a few times. There wasn't much love between the girls and their old roommate. She always seemed to come by when she wanted something: a can of tomato sauce or ten dollars or to borrow the plunger. Sally warned Spider that Tara was fucked up. She didn't care much for her either way but Blue couldn't seem to stand her. Spider once asked, "Why do you talk to her then?"

"Because," Blue had stated, "it's good to keep your enemies close. Girls are excellent at warfare!"

Tara had dyed hair and thinly-plucked eyebrows. Her skin was pale, she wore heavy makeup, and always had a cigarette in her mouth. She disliked the company of girls while presenting herself as bisexual. Tara had a smiling panel of fairies tattooed on her back, but her eyes were lonely and cold. There was never a shortage of boys around her.

"Why are you asking about Tara, Pot-Kid?"

"You've got a crush on her!"

Sally groaned. "Why does every single guy have to think with his dink?"

"Guys always want what they don't have," said Blue. "Why do you think they're so fascinated with tits?"

The next day Sally came home with some weed she'd been given that was still too wet to smoke. "Roll up a joint and put it in

dirtbags > 25

the microwave for seven seconds," Spider said. "It'll come out perfectly dry." Someone knocked and Blue let Tara in, rolling her eyes.

"Look at this—it's Betty Whattabake and Martha McMuffin," she said when the timer beeped. Sally ignored her and rolled the joint while Blue changed the station on the radio.

"'Lick the sky'? What does that *mean*? It makes me think of people who need to take a bath!" Spider held the joint out to Tara. "No THANK you," she sniffed.

"That's Tara for you," Blue said. "She doesn't smoke weed. But she'll steal your boyfriend."

"Hah," Tara said. "I don't smoke weed because people who are stoned laugh at things that aren't funny."

"What's wrong with laughing at everything?"

"Sally?" Tara said, exasperated.

"*I* like to see people having a good time!"

"Yeah," Spider jumped in. "What's the problem here?"

Tara made a face. "Look, I just came by to borrow some toilet paper. Just gimme it and I'll get out of this estro-den." They gave her half a roll and she left. "See you around Spider," she cooed, wiggling her tits at the door.

Tara came by again the next week. Blue had a late shift and Sally was out drinking with Angelica, and Angelica's youngest sister, a hot lesbian who flipped burgers at Hooters. Spider wanted to take a long, hot bath. Smoking in the tub was a dirty pleasure she enjoyed. She heard Tara in the hallway calling her name.

"I want you to go out with me tonight," Tara said, barging in when Spider opened the door. She'd already phoned twice from upstairs. "I've been at the clinic all day. I just had my second abortion. I need to party tonight," Tara said. "Fucking party."

Spider considered which was worse: Tara drinking or Tara drinking alone. She agreed to go with her to a bar downtown. Tara paid for the cab. As they sat in the bar and drank Spider asked, "What about the...guy?"

"Huh?"

"The father," Spider said.

"I think it was the guy who left a note the next morning that said, 'Sorry, the condom broke.'" They were pretty drunk when Tara said, "Can I sleep over tonight? The doctor told me I should stay with someone." Spider couldn't refuse, but didn't really want to say yes.

"I want another DRINK!" Tara yelled later, as the bar was about to close. They were long out of money and had no way home. Desperate men began to look for someone to pick up; they circled the bar like vultures. Spider knew one of them was their only way home. The guy who had been standing next to her turned and said, "I can flip a dump truck with my tongue."

He had a mischievous smile and Spider took the cue. "If you buy a six-pack and pay for the cab you can come over," she said. The boy readily agreed. They got a taxi and somehow Spider ended up in the front with the driver. "You're taking the wrong streets," she yelled at the cabbie, even though she had no idea where she was going.

Spider looked in the back seat. Tara and the boy sat closely together. When they got to her place they drank the beer and Tara went to take a bath. Spider and the boy smoked a joint and passed out curled up on the couch.

She woke up later alone and heard something in the dark. It was Tara and the boy. They were having sex on the floor. It was horrible hearing them like that, the sloppy wet sounds and groans. Without thinking Spider yelled, "Shut up!"

"Spider?" Tara's voice sounded tiny and far away. Spider went to sleep in her own room, uneasy and disgusted.

The next day she told Blue what had happened. "Forget her," Blue said. "Take a good look and then stay away from *that* mess."

5

Crispy invited them to a smoke-filled coffee house for his first poetry reading. Spider, Sally, and Blue crammed on one of the couches in the back. Before it started Crispy split a few grams of chocolate-covered mushrooms with them in secret from his girlfriend, a short, white-knuckled girl in a severe black dress. The open mic started and a few flakes got up and read their poetry. It was mostly dull and long-winded, with quite a few hippie rants.

"This is horrible," Sally said. She seemed to be in physical pain.

"Quiet," Blue said. "Next up is Aurora Celeste!"

A woman recited moon poems and moaned into the microphone. The mushrooms made everything twinkle. Spider couldn't stop giggling at the rigid look of horror on Sally's face. It was her first poetry reading and Spider suspected it would be her last. Then Crispy took his turn onstage and introduced himself.

"My name is Dallas Firestorm," he said. "This is my first piece. Untitled." He pulled his pants down and bent over. Crispy had declined to wear underwear that evening. "Eat my bum, Mom!" he screamed. "Big Mac in my poo!"

Crispy's girlfriend rushed out of the room when the host asked him to leave the stage. Sally gave a standing ovation. Crispy chased after his girlfriend and came back inconsolable when she'd dumped him on the street. He vowed to stop smoking pot for the next two weeks.

"It was the best thing for him," Sally said after he left. "That girl had the sense of humour of a cop."

Spider agreed. "She was a talking golf ball!"

"We should throw her a surprise party," Blue said. "We'll dig a hole, and put a rug over it, and when she falls into it we'll yell 'Surprise!' and start to party."

Their cackles took over the room.

Summer was almost over. The hot sun made Spider want to drink beer, be outside moving, slowing down and speeding up with the waves of heat. There were almost perfect moments, when the ocean air felt clean and there was a good song on the radio, and she smoked a cigarette with something like reverence. It felt like anything could happen as she walked down the street, sandy and sunburned. The hours of a Friday night fell easily away.

Blue and Spider sat in the kitchen one night, even drunker than usual. They'd started drinking at the CC Saloon in the afternoon and Sally was still there. "How come you never talk about your brother?" Blue asked suddenly.

Spider's heart beat so fast her chest felt like it was vibrating. "It's hard to talk about," she said. "What kind of question is that?"

"Spider, I'm sorry." It was obvious Blue meant it.

"You wanna know? I'll tell you. There's this feeling of numbness. Things happen around you—conversations, interactions ... but you don't really feel a part of them. And now it's like I don't ever remember not feeling this way. It's fucking painful. That's why I can't talk about my brother. *Get* it?"

Blue got up to leave and Spider could tell her feelings were hurt. "Wait," she said. And suddenly Spider did want to tell her about Johnny. The past flowed over her hot and bright. She began to talk about the visits to her uncle's farm on weekends when they had to put on a new barn roof or build another room for the babies that kept coming. Sometimes other relatives drove out. The kids played with the horse and the pigs or roamed in the junkyard of old cars by the river. The men drank beer and worked and the aunties smoked their long cigarettes in the kitchen and played cards before starting on dinner. Johnny organized games that all the cousins could play, even the little ones. He'd divide them into war camps defending terrain, or as different tribes on scouting missions exploring in the woods. He made the whole day fun at the farm and those were the best times Spider could remember.

"Johnny was really good with kids," she said.

Spider got up and stumbled to bed. She wouldn't cry until she was under the covers with the pillow over her head.

6

The song went, *the years go fast and the days go so slow*. Spider got up and staggered to the bathroom. It was Sunday morning and they were out of toilet paper. Blue brought her a coffee filter. "We like to call this the hiney grind," she said in a cool British tone. Sally Pepper sounded demented as she laughed behind the door.

A horn honked outside and Spider threw on some sneakers.

She wore black jeans and a black T-shirt, her hair in two fat braids. At the door she relented and took off her dark sunglasses. She was going to the beach with a boy named Fergus Finn. Fergus drove a blue van. "Hey tough girl," he said when she got in. He'd packed a box of cookies and three grams of mushrooms in a lunchbox.

They'd met at the CC Saloon a few nights before. Fergus had kept waving at her across the room. Finally Spider had walked over. "Yeah?"

"You dropped something," he'd said, and held out a piece of paper.

"What?"

"My phone number."

It had turned out Fergus knew Sally through a guy named Frank, who lived in a house with Sally's friend, Bigfoot. Sally and Bigfoot had gone to high school together, pulling schemes and trading punches. For years they'd just been friends, but they had a strange relationship. Once in a while a cute and brave boy developed a crush on Sally and Bigfoot found some reason to beat him up. Sally would be really angry for a while then she'd give the boy a smile with her chipped front teeth that made him like her all over again.

At a bus stop a pear-shaped man staggered up from the bench, legs like tiny chicken wings beneath the shadow of his stomach. Spider pointed him out to Fergus and they had a good laugh. He lit a joint smoothly without taking his eyes off the road. His sandy blonde hair was messy and he had a small gap between his front teeth that made him look like an excited kid.

Fergus had hurt his leg racing dirt bikes. He walked with a wooden cane that had a silver bike bell attached and because of this Spider liked him.

"I just came back from my friend Kevin's funeral," Fergus

said. "Kev the dirtbag," he said. "He drove his car drunk into a school bus."

"Oh god," Spider said, picturing bloody, mangled children. "That's horrible."

"Everyone was fine," Fergus assured her.

Spider looked out the window. "Well, everyone except Kevin."

At the beach they walked slowly, up small hills and over rocks. Finally they spread out a blanket in a secluded spot. The ocean was beautiful and the day was warm. There was almost no one else around and Spider stretched out. The sound of the waves were peaceful. They smoked a joint and the afternoon began to pass, happily stoned. Just when she thought *this is nice* Fergus put his hand on the inside of her thigh. It seemed to be a move considered a few times before its execution. He said he liked to fuck outside. Spider didn't really want to, but his friend had just died. Fergus murmured into her ear. The hot sun beat her down.

Afterwards they ate the cookies. And the psychedelics. And rats came out of the driftwood.

7

Fergus Finn had a short attention span and a wise-cracking mouth. He worked the phone at a company selling resort time to rich Americans, and as soon as he got paid he blew his load on a few nights of heavy partying. Spider admired the ferocity of his benders. He gobbled any drug he could get his hands on and drank triple rye whiskies, straight. Mushrooms were eaten by the handful, so drunk he could barely chew, and when he took acid it had to be four hits at a time. Spider met a lot of people who forgot her name.

Most nights she went home before anything happened. There was a small window of time to get with Fergus, between the middle of his last beer and before he passed out. Spider would watch him get drunker and drunker until she knew she'd lost him for the night. Usually he'd black out early on after doing things that were stupid and rarely funny, like taking an old man's hat or climbing up a drainpipe of a building just to piss off the roof, or flashing a girl on the bus.

Fergus always called to apologize. Then he'd ask, "What did I do?"

"You pushed over a girl on crutches."

"Really?"

"Then you took a shit on someone's lawn."

"I did? HAW HAW!" He enjoyed himself so much sometimes Spider didn't bother telling him when it wasn't true.

Fergus Finn lived in block apartments in an area that had become a middle-class Chinese ghetto. In front of the building a chain link fence surrounded a tiny patch of grass too dead to call a lawn. It had been what she'd expected; greasy kitchen walls and one stinky towel in the bathroom. His roommate was a muscle-head who showed up at home only to yell at his girlfriend over the phone before going back to her place to yell in person.

Fergus came to her window almost every night that September. Sometimes his friend Frank came too. She'd hear them late at night with their strange calls that sounded like barking dogs. Frank was good-looking, funny and crude, and when Spider didn't know what to laugh off she stayed quiet. In the mornings her mascara left black smears across the pillow. If

dirtbags > 33

Spider stayed with Fergus she always wished she were home in her own bed. He breathed with his mouth open. Sometimes their hands curled together in sleep. For a moment it would be sweet but Spider was always hung-over, wanting to puke from the taste in her mouth.

He convinced Spider to come to the tiny bar bathroom. Fergus had a smile that had gotten him by his whole life. Her skirt was up and panties down, a sudden star, the stage as big as a toilet. She fucked his mouth with her tongue, climbed on the sink while his body cocked like a gun in her hot, wet fists. Spider watched their reflection in the mirror. Someone outside banged on the door and she thought, *I have begun to do bad things.*

Last call came and Fergus had disappeared. She and Frank looked for him. "He probably wandered off somewhere to smoke a joint," Frank said. They waited outside for a while and then Spider stopped a cab. Frank jumped in, too.

"I'm going home, Frank."

"I just need to use your phone," he said. When they got inside Blue and Sally were already in bed. "Let's smoke some weed," Frank said and leaned across her on the couch to dump his pot pipe in the ashtray.

The window wouldn't close. The cold air blew in and Frank told Spider all the times he had driven by to see if she was home, if she was alone.

He said, "You don't even *know*."

Spider felt that in her cunt. She stood up and told him to go.

Frank told Fergus the night he and Spider left the bar together she was so drunk she tried to fuck him in the living room. Fergus repeated this to her over the phone. Sally said he knew what Frank said wasn't true, but they were best friends and there was nothing he could do. Spider stormed sixteen blocks over to his place.

He let her in and she saw that Frank was there, too. A wrestling match blared from the TV and they ignored her. She pictured Frank at the air vent listening when she and Fergus were fucking. "You're disgusting," she told him. The fans on TV cheered wildly.

Frank said, "Don't fire up on me!"

Fergus still wouldn't look at her and she snapped. "Fergus, you *know* nothing happened with him."

"What's done is done," Fergus said, but then his voice got louder. "Why do all the girls I meet HAVE TO FUCK my filthiest friend?"

"Hey man," Frank said.

"It didn't happen!" Spider walked to the door. She was so angry she felt herself freeze over inside and then she was very calm. "Fuck you, Frank. You're *garbage*."

"Ha ha," Frank laughed. It sounded hollow. Fergus was looking at her now.

"And fuck YOU Fergus," she said. "From now on you'll get more love from a hooker than from me."

Spider slammed the door as hard as she could. Then she stood on the corner and waited to see if Fergus would come. She kind of thought he would, but he didn't.

8

The weed was long gone and Spider needed work. She'd borrowed money from her parents but that was spent. Sally assured her she would starve to death before welfare kicked in.

Spider asked Blue to lend her a dress, and woke up early three days in a row. She took the first job she got, a waitress in a Chinese restaurant. "Are you fast, fast, fast?" the owner asked, looking her up and down with doubt. Spider assured him that yes, she was that fast. She lasted a week and thought that was something because the owner kept following her back and forth from the kitchen to yell at her slowness.

After taking a typing test she worked a few days a week as an office girl. Spider couldn't stand the clothes she had to wear and the only thing she liked about the job was lunch. Everyone in the office reminded her of slugs—grey, moist, and slow moving. It felt too similar to university with the endless bureaucracy and paper pushing.

She took her resume to a bookstore in her neighbourhood. Ralph, the owner, was a retired navy man with three ex-wives. Spider was anxious and bit her thumb while he looked over her resume. "You've been to university," he said. He didn't sound very impressed. Ralph was balding on top and had a gut he had given up trying to control.

"Don't hold it against me," she said. Small flowers of wrinkles sprung up beside Ralph's eyes when he smiled. He said she could start the next week.

Spider's co-worker Connie looked like she had been smoking since she was four. Connie had cut her hours to part-time because her daughter was back in rehab and she had to take care of her autistic grandchild. When Ralph was gone she sent Spider on coffee runs and let her leave early. Connie was a pro and saved the crossword puzzle to do when it wasn't busy. There was a bakery next door and all day long the bookstore smelled like cinnamon buns. Spider felt like things were finally looking up.

When she got her first paycheque she took Blue out for drinks to celebrate. They sat on the patio at the CC Saloon drinking spicy Caesars. The waitress and Blue had a twenty-dollar bet they wouldn't smoke cigarettes all night. Spider noticed a girl by the bar staring at her. When she saw Spider looking she walked over and said, "You know, Fergus was only *using* you for sex." The girl had crispy brown hair and small, sharp teeth. She looked like a wolverine.

Spider leaned back in her seat. "I've always been pretty lucky," she drawled. The girl twisted her lips and walked away. Blue roared with laughter.

"Nice one," she said.

"Don't let it bother you," the waitress said. She sat down with her tray and started to work her way through a menthol. "Men will fuck *mud*."

Spider shrugged and lit a cigarette. Later on she lit a whole lot more.

9

The rain in Vancouver lasted all winter. Spider made just enough at the bookstore to survive and lived one paycheque to the next. The nights with Sally and Blue were a stream of free drinks and red lights that left her with a sore belly, a nasty cough some mornings. Yet it was hard to calm the feeling of wanting to roam the city. She kept a smooth black crystal in her pocket and worked it over and over with her thumb.

Spider's mother phoned late in the evening, talking about her prescription medications. She said a lot of things in her phone call and not many of them were good. Blue got calls from Gerda who told her to be careful, that they lived in strange and dangerous times. Blue organized her closet, painted designs on her bedroom walls. Spider wanted bags of drugs to kill everything inside her.

They spent the twelve days of Christmas at the CC Saloon. Outside, the city turned dull grey. On and on it rained.

10

Blue recited the names of endangered birds while they watched the *National Geographic* channel. "Broad-winged Hawk, Whooping Crane, Pleated Woodpecker..."

"That just proves that the world is a terrible place," Sally complained. "Shaddup!" The January rain seemed endless and no one wanted to be outside. Spider and Sally grumbled in the living room. Blue wouldn't let anyone use the phone. She was waiting for a call from the new boy who had just started as a bus boy in Sally's restaurant.

"He's good-looking and basically useless," Sally said. "He's a CIRCUS PONY!" Blue ignored her.

The phone rang and Spider grabbed it. She felt giddy and weird from lack of sunlight. "Just a second, Shooter," she said, and fired a pistol finger at Blue. Sally cackled and Blue lunged at the phone. She made obscene gestures at them while cooing into the receiver. When she hung up Blue informed Sally and Spider that they were being kicked out for the evening.

"Tonight's the night," Blue said. "I'm gonna tell him, 'Get dinner while it's hot!'"

Sally went to the store for a bottle of gin; she and Spider sat and got nicely drunk. Blue had given her the money and Sally had even gotten limes. Finally the bottle was finished. "Okay," Blue said. "You bitches take a hike!"

It had stopped raining so they decided to walk downtown and save money. "Goddamn Blue," Sally said. "She kicked us to the curb. I hope he gets coffee table cock!"

"What's that?"

"When his dick doesn't work and sits like a useless piece of wood between them!"

"Well, she did give us drinking money," Spider said, pulling the strap on her bag. She'd learned to take everything with her when she went out for the night—keys, makeup, money, sunglasses. They went into a café but the waiter wouldn't give up the bathroom key so they went into the alley and peed by the dumpster. It smelled like the piss of a hundred other people.

"Don't dally...Sally," Spider sang. It felt good to be outside. On the way to the bar they smoked a joint. Inside they sat with

Angelica, who was stoned and fingering her corduroy purse. She hardly ever smiled and when she did her face looked stretched and unused. Sally came back with some drinks and pushed aside some coats to slide in. "How're things, Angelica?"

"I'm *sooo* over Jude," she said. "I hardly cry about him anymore."

Every time the waitress came by Angelica whispered to Spider, "Get another, get another." Then she slipped her hand over Spider's mouth, her thumb pushing a small capsule between her lips. Spider held it on her tongue for a second or two. Everyone else swallowed their pill so she did, too.

Soon after Spider began to see weird flashes of coloured lights. She noticed people with sores in the corner of their mouths and the drummer from the band looking across the bar at her like a stalker. The air was a horrible, hot stink and her chest began closing up. Angelica leaned over, her skin a sick green and yellow. She put her face up close and kept asking, "Are you okay? Are you okay?" Then Spider really felt the drugs kick in.

There was a car ride, and then she was in a room full of shiny people in a chemical trance. Spider sat with one eye closed, looking at the people in the party. After awhile she switched to the other eye. She thought of the good times with Fergus, and how he had dumped her. It felt like being sliced open with a roughly cut diamond.

Sally was talking to a group of people across the room and obviously enjoying herself. Spider felt queasy at the chemically earnest love. Every response she made seemed a second too late. She tried to calm herself, afraid she might start to gnaw her lips or spit. The squealing underage girls made her feel self-conscious and bitter. Spider knew with that attitude she had no business being there. She looked around the party and realized every single person was having a good time but her. All the love she'd been given felt long used up. The girl next to her pulled her braids so her head moved side to side, her eyes two shiny black orbs. Her friend said, "I love to meet people! I love it! It's so exciting! Loving people, liking people. *Hating*. I just get so excited! I love it! I love it! I love it!"

"Things move in circles that are too wide and ugly to comprehend," Spider told them. "Can you try to understand that?"

She pushed through the crowd and got her coat. In the video monitors she could see the kids dance. Some guy wearing blue sunglasses stopped her at the door. "You are on a very dark ride," he said.

"Fuck you, shit-flaps!"

Sally came over and put her arm around Spider's shoulder. "No head butts tonight," she chuckled. They walked outside and stood on the street. Spider flicked a cigarette into an open Explorer. It began to smolder on the black leather seat. Her eyes grew dark like a terrible storm.

"Let's go find some trouble," she said.

It was dark. Spider woke up lying clothed on a strange bed. For a long time she just lay there, twitching. She imagined she had developed cerebral palsy. Pieces of the night floated slowly together; leaving another party and piling into a car, her legs so squished she began to shriek and Sally telling her to calm down; stopping at one house and then Angelica's, stumbling room to room; strange faces hunched over lines of powders; moving in quick bursts of motion that made her sick.

The door opened and Sally stood there with Spider's bag. "Are you o*kay*?"

"I'm lying here twitching," she croaked. "In my own personal hell."

It was the first time Spider had ever seen Sally look worried. "Maybe you should slow down," she said gently. "Darlin', this isn't a race."

dirtbags > 41

11

Crispy had stopped coming by the apartment after the weed ran out. The girls sat and discussed it. "He never calls anymore," Spider complained. "What happened to him?"

"Didn't you hear? He's dating Tara."

"Noooooo!"

Blue shook her head. "You've lost him to the void."

"I miss him, too," Sally said. "But he'll be back. It won't take long for him to figure out she's crazy nut-bark." She made double circles around her ears for emphasis.

"But why doesn't he still come by?"

"Trust me," Sally said. "It would piss Tara off to the point of violence."

"Yeah," Blue agreed. "It would be nuclear fucking winter."

Spider felt better. It had saddened her to think their friendship was based solely on the fact they smoked pot.

Crispy re-appeared on Valentine's Day with a pocketful of chocolate eggs. "Pot-Kid's back," Sally yelled when she opened the door. "Where's the Sea Hag?" she asked, referring to Tara's recently dyed-green hair. He admitted he'd been seeing her but their relationship was over.

Sally packed another bowl while Crispy told them how she'd thrown a toaster at his head. It had missed so she'd launched a chair and bruised his rib cage instead. When he'd tried to break up with Tara over the phone she'd come over and tried to kick in his door screaming, so he'd sent her an email instead.

"Now you're going to have to make commando runs in and out of the building," Sally sympathized. Crispy cracked his knuckles and began a vigorous session of neck calisthenics.

Crispy wanted to see a band but Sally had to work so only Spider came. He said he would buy her drinks all night as long as they were scotch. Pretty soon she was ridiculously drunk.

Spider asked a boy if he wanted to play pool. She swayed and put the wrong end of the cigarette in her mouth. He said, "I'm with the BAND," like she was some kind of groupie. They started playing and she tried to ignore them but they were too good so she just gave up and started dancing.

After the show ended Crispy said he knew a party where the band might play afterward. They went around the corner and he pulled out a joint. "Do you ever miss Tara," Spider asked, "even though she's somewhat insane?"

"Sometimes I long for her," he said honestly. "I thought we had something good for a while."

"I never think about my ex-boyfriends," Spider said. It was almost true, since when they slipped into her head she pushed them straight out. "Each one was an asshole, but in his own unique way."

"Don't dog brand my whole gender," Crispy said. "You're ripped!"

"I'm wasted," Spider agreed, and leaned in to kiss him. "Why did we never get together?"

Crispy said, "Because you're like my sexy little brother!" He grinned and pulled down her cap so it covered her eyes.

An old toothless guy came up and said he was an artist so they sparked the joint and let him smoke it, too. The bum lectured them about wasting time. Then he told Spider he liked her ass and wanted to roll it around some paint on a canvas. He sounded like he was really into it. After he toddled off Spider told Crispy, "I might have considered it, if he'd had at least a FEW teeth. Maybe he has a friend."

"Great," Crispy said. "You could make a big yuck sandwich."

dirtbags > 43

The party was in a nice two-storey house occupied by three horrible women. The kitchen was too bright and everyone smiled like sharks. Spider had a couple of beers and then found a couple more. When the band arrived she talked to the bass player. He was cute and wore a brown derby and ate a huge slab of cake with his hands. An unsmiling girl in leather came into the kitchen and stood beside him. She began to rub his shoulder while slowly sizing Spider up with a look that said she wasn't much.

Spider thought the party was still going on in the living room but when she got there the room was empty. She stared at a velvet painting, too sick to even smoke another cigarette. Crispy had long since disappeared and her hands hung uselessly. She wondered if she could just curl up on the couch for a moment and then someone yelled, "Go home!" It was like a firecracker hit her and she went straight for the door.

12

Her mother phoned to say happy birthday. Spider had just come home from work and was about to light a spliff when she called. When she heard her mother's voice a feeling came over Spider like a tidal wave. She put the joint down and sighed.

"I saw Mrs. Newton in the grocery store," her mother said. Dave had flown his mother to Arizona for a golf holiday. She went on and on. "You had a good catch there with that one."

Spider said, "Mom, your concepts are really gross." *And Dave grows weed with his criminal brother*, she wanted to add.

"You're not getting any younger."

"I am TWENTY-TWO years old."

"How could you go to university for two years and not find a husband?"

"Jesus! Lay off me. Christ, I don't want to hear this shit."

"I'm your mother. I worry about you."

"Look," said Spider. "I have to go. Thanks for calling."

"There's boxes of your things here," her mother said. "What do you want me to do with them?" Spider tried to think of what that would be—clothes, yearbooks, a stuffed animal or two. She wished she had something gentle to say to her mother.

"Toss it," she said.

Sally and Blue sat outside on their packs and waited for the taxi to drive them to the bus depot. They had applied and gotten summer jobs at a fishing lodge. The pay was huge because it was isolated on a tiny Gulf island. Sally had to work in the kitchen but Blue had gotten an easy job at the front desk. Spider hadn't sent her application in on time and all the positions were taken.

The girls would be at the lodge for two and a half months and Blue had hooked up some visiting Swedes to sublet the apartment the entire time they were gone. Spider moved into Sally's room and the Swedes shared Blue's. The tiny closet room stayed empty.

Spider watched Sally and Blue sadly. She knew she'd have a lonely summer without them.

"Don't you goddamn cry," Blue warned. Everyone knew she hated Christmas and greeting cards, and that most of all she hated goodbyes.

"Here," Spider said as she held out a shopping bag. "I packed you guys treats for the bus."

"Oh my god," Sally squealed. "Cigarettes, animal crackers, a lighter, *High Times*—that's mine!—two scratch tickets...and a bag of corn nuts!" Sally gave her a hug. "Now *I'm* gonna cry."

"What am I going to without you guys?" Spider put her hand over her mouth and looked down at her feet.

"Spider, you'll be *fine*," Blue said. "You're the sweetest badass we know."

Spider liked working in the bookstore. She found the order and structure calmed her. On sunny days after work she took a blanket to the park and read. When she wasn't at work Spider could go whole days without speaking to anyone. She tried to convince herself that she could live on very little affection. The Swedes were beautiful girls, clean, cold, and rarely home.

One evening after work Spider saw Fergus on the bus. He didn't have his cane anymore. She couldn't find the energy to still be angry, and once Fergus sensed that he was charming and sweet. They didn't talk about Frank, or anything that had happened before. They were way past that now. He asked if she wanted to have a drink with him and she agreed. The Swedes were gone for the weekend to hike some mountain. Spider didn't want to be alone while the whole summer slipped away.

She and Fergus spent a few nights together. In the morning one of them always made an excuse to leave. It was a given that nothing be serious between them. A phone call from Fergus meant a good time. She made him breakfast in the mornings. He put Louisiana hot sauce on everything he ate.

But as the summer passed more and more Spider liked his boy room, with the milk crates full of records and greasy skateboard wheels on the floor. Fergus had been through a hard childhood and hadn't been given much love. In the moments when he was sweet she could see how hard he tried.

Spider called Fergus a few times and he didn't call back. He had moved into a house but she didn't like phoning there because none of his roommates were very friendly, especially one dread-locked girl who rode a BMX and always sounded cryptic. Spider rode over to his place on her bike. No one was around except a guy who was a friend of a friend, playing guitar on the front porch with a cat at his feet. "Fergus hasn't been around for a few days," he told her. "I don't know where he is."

"I hope he's okay," Spider said. Right away she regretted it because the look on the boy's face was a mixture of disbelief and pity. Spider said goodbye and hurried away.

She knew it was over. The reasons she'd once liked Fergus—his casual nature and easy affection—were the things she began to despise. There wasn't a phone number for Sally and Blue at the fishing lodge, and in a way Spider was glad she couldn't call them. She'd seen Fergus coming a mile away and hadn't even swerved.

13

When Sally and Blue got home Spider felt like part of the city again. She'd made a pie for them she presented after they'd kicked out the Swedes. Spider stood in the middle of the dismantled kitchen with the plate in her hands. "The meringue didn't work out." It was a cliché but her mother really *had* made it look so easy.

Blue was suntanned and her hair had grown out into a long pixie cut. She looked like a forest sprite with lipstick and glorious tits. The pie was placed on the coffee table between a bag of weed, a container of tiger balm, a pot of lukewarm coffee, and two lighters. They stared at the smooth matte surface of the pie.

"Without the meringue it seems nude," Sally said.

"You're right. It looks obscene."

"Fuck that meringue shit!" Blue barked from her reclined position on the floor. "Let's just eat the motherfucker!" It seemed that Blue's tremendous capacity for foul language had somehow gotten even bigger in the forest.

Sally showed Spider the giant red blisters on her hands and told battle stories of the insane kitchen crew. Working at the lodge had been grueling, but she had come back to the city with almost six grand. "It should fund our drinking for at *least* two months," Blue said.

The girls had stories. To her own disbelief, Sally had made out with a cute hippie boy who didn't even know how to kiss. Blue had developed an intense feeling for a blue-eyed bush cook with magic hands. They went camping together and she told Spider in a hushed voice that he'd washed her with water from the canteen.

Sally had brought back some organic weed and they passed her pipe. Spider had to admit the pie was truly horrible. "I've never been much for baking," she said. "Let's go get ice cream."

"And liquor," Sally added. "I can't drink as much now. It takes awhile to re-tox!"

"Bring me something back," Blue said, and fingered the ghost of her nose ring.

Spider was stoned and startled by the bright sunlight. A homeless man sat cross-legged on a folded carpet in a doorway, reading a newspaper. A kinky-haired boy strumming his guitar wandered after them then turned around when someone else caught his eye. Two boys threw water balloons at the Catholic church. The puddles smelled like clean rain.

They heard the sound of a barking dog and bongo drums. A group of young squeegee punks shuffled on the corner. A female cop ripped through a knapsack, flinging its contents. "Keep it up and you'll go to the drunk tank," she told a girl in gum boots and a camouflage skirt. The girl looked angry and sober.

Spider thought about it, but nothing much had really changed while Blue and Sally were gone. The old hangouts were still there. Angelica was back with Jude the Dirtbag. Crispy had started hanging with computer tech-heads and a splinter group of hacker terrorists. There was a new DJ at the Quarry, and he wasn't as good as Mandy. Tara was dating the gayest straight man in Vancouver. Spider's favourite old building, down by the bookstore, was being torn down to build another condo.

At the ice cream shop they looked in the cases until Sally decided on chocolate amaretto and got an ice cream sandwich for Blue. Sally took a giant lick of her cone. She looked like a little kid and it made Spider feel a sudden, overwhelming love for her friend. Finally she ordered lemon gelato.

"Good choice," Sally said. "Lemon tastes good on a sunny day."

They walked home down the other side of the street. Past a boarded up jazz club, some vegetable stalls, a car lot. They cut down an alley past a group of men crowded outside the back door of a bar. Spider slowed down. Sally said something she didn't hear and kept walking.

A balding man stood in the middle of the half-circle with his pants down. A worn-looking woman with coarse blonde hair knelt in front of him on the rough cement. The air smelled like hot oil and Chinese food cooking. One of the men watching said, "She's sucking him off!" The guy beside him said, "You can count the stretch marks around her mouth." The woman looked up smiling at the crowd. Her eyes shone like black opals. Spider turned and ran from those sounds, that woman, the ugly red cock in her mouth. Sally was already at the church when she caught up. They walked over water splashes and bits of balloon.

"Christ Sally, what the fuck was *that*?"

"I didn't see a thing," Sally said. "It's gonna be a banner year!"

Spider's mouth tasted like sour lemon. She looked at the cone in her hand. At the next garbage can she threw it away.

14

Fergus bumped into Spider on a sidewalk in her neighbourhood. It was September and the front yards were covered in gold and red leaves.

"Hey tough girl," Fergus said. He held a bottle of fireball whisky and didn't have a carefree look anymore.

"What's new, Fergus?"

"I'm moving to Edmonton in two weeks," he said.

Spider was surprised she didn't like the idea of the city without him. "Why are you going there?"

"Moving back."

"Why?"

Fergus shrugged. "I don't know."

"What are you doing now?"

Fergus shrugged again. There was an element of secrecy to all her ex-boyfriends Spider found unnerving.

"Let's go to work on that bottle."

They went back to her place since she knew no one was home. Fergus told stories and clowned around, Spider laughed at his jokes. For a while it felt like old times. She remembered how she used to look for his van out the window when she knew he was coming over. Then Fergus decided to give himself a tattoo. Rat bones. He pulled out a blue *BiC* and heated the end of a safety pin. Spider realized with a sad clarity that what she had loved about Fergus was the way he surprised her—how he danced, or that he spoke Gaelic, or would pull his hat down over his eyes in a loud bar and holler. Most surprising to her was that he'd given up so easily. The pin got hotter. He shoved the tip into the skin above his elbow, jabbed again and again. More ink, more jabs. Spider watched his face. He wouldn't flinch.

"I blew it with you," Fergus said. "Like I always knew I would."

Spider found herself walking the streets alone, trying not to look in the eyes of everyone she passed; young girls in tight pants; old men in faded coats and polished shoes; a hunchback laden with grocery bags at a bus stop with no bench. And then there were the junkies, always waiting. The idea of the winter days ahead felt like fingers of panic tightening around Spider's bones.

Loneliness began to creep across her skin like barnacles.

15

On the walk downtown they passed a woman twitching on the front steps of a run-down house. "*She* didn't get her cheque today," said Tara, who had managed to invite herself for drinks. She had re-dyed her hair and now made a grotesque amount of money as a hostess in a yuppie eatery.

Blue said. "It's not just a Wednesday. It's *welfare* Wednesday."

"It's Mardis Gras!" Sally said. "AND we have money."

They agreed going to the bar without having to steal drinks or hustle made it easier to look people in the eye. Sally and Blue had enough money now and didn't need to rent out the closet room, but they insisted Spider stay on. Spider was relieved because she didn't want to leave and couldn't afford to move anyway. It alarmed her that she'd gotten so attached to her home.

"Things can always be worse," Spider said.

"I'll tell you what that is," Blue said, pointing her small finger. "That's the cry of the terminally doomed!"

They walked fast and swung their hips. A group of boys on skateboards rode past, then a girl on a painted-up Raleigh, knees pumping, ass and chin in the air. At the CC Saloon they decided to sit outside. Spider sipped a beer and watched an old drunk with dirty fingernails tilt his face to the sun.

Blue posed with her Virginia Slim as she poured raw whisky down her throat. She pointed out Fergus Finn sitting at a table on the other side of the patio. Spider had admitted to the girls she'd re-dated him that summer.

"I don't want you to let this bother you too much," Sally said. "But Fergus is known for being—" she paused and took a gulp of beer—"a notorious male slut."

"Don't take boys like him seriously," Blue said. "When one leaves, just go find another."

"*Forget* him," Sally said. "He's dirty. Every once in awhile one slips under the radar."

They ordered another pitcher of beer and drank. At the back of the bar Blue played pool with a bearded man in a leather jacket. When he lost the game he picked up his cel phone and threatened to have her killed.

They left in a hurry and ended up down the street at the Whistling Elephant, a dive bar that featured karaoke with a live band. A crusted-over buffet stood gelling in the corner near the pinball machines. Darlene, the ancient owner, shuffled back and forth behind the counter, wig dipping slightly over her left eye. Her much younger husband, sixty at least, wore Hawaiian shirts and stood by the entrance, flirting with underage girls. Spider, Sally, and Blue slid into a red vinyl booth and watched the band, who all seemed too drunk to play. A guy finished his karaoke song then walked up to their table. "I just finished my set," he said. "But I'll be back in twenty minutes."

Sally went for the first round. Darlene was so old she'd often forget how much she charged for drinks. A pint of beer could cost fifty cents or five dollars. Arguing with Darlene was pointless and angered her to a fit. It was a gamble everyone accepted.

Sally came back with three drinks in her hands. "I got off easy," she said. "Darlene thinks it's 1965!"

Spider caught Fergus staring from the corner, and he smiled. She felt like there was no bottom to her stomach. Blue shook her fist and he turned away.

"Fergus followed you here," Sally said. "Can you believe that?"

"I HATE those guys," Blue said, and elaborated: boys who called late at night and left vague messages, who were always broke and borrowed money they never paid back, who tried to fuck as many girls as they could and traveled in a sneering pack with others just like them.

"That's the problem when you go out with a joker," Sally said. "They know the right way to treat you. They just think it's funnier not to."

Spider had to pass by Fergus on the way to the bathroom. She stopped and said, "I thought you were leaving town."

He kissed her cheek. "I'll miss you," he said. He smelled like sweat and beer and there was a look in his eyes that confused her.

"Uh…I gotta go pee," Spider said. She sat in the bathroom stall feeling like an idiot. A group of girls came in. One put her arms in the air and yelled "I'm gonna get laid. TONIGHT!" Everyone stopped pushing each other at the mirror to cheer.

Spider came out of the bathroom and saw Blue dancing on the table. A bunch of people crowded in front of her. "C'mon!" she yelled drunkenly to Spider. "We're taking the party home!"

"What about the neighbours?"

"Fuck the neighbours! Tonight, WE MAKE PARTY!"

Fergus was at her side. "I'm coming too," he said. "Okay?" Spider drained the last of her beer and staggered out. Blue pushed her into a taxi without him. Traces of Fergus lingered, none of them good. Blue told Spider every reason not to trust boys and the taxi ride home with strangers was hell.

Inside the apartment people crowded against each other. Someone turned the stereo up too loud. Fergus came with a car full of people, Tara giggling on his arm. Spider slumped against the fridge, holding a can of beer she didn't want to drink. Fergus leaned in and stuck his sour-tasting tongue in her mouth. Spider went to the bathroom and puked, then gulped water from the sink.

Sally kicked Fergus out and one by one everyone left but a girl with feathered hair and a pot belly. She paged her coke-dealing boyfriend three times then pulled out a flap and they did fat lines on the coffee table until he came to pick her up. "All this just to feel normal," Spider said.

Her boyfriend's tattoos were crude. When he said, "Let's party," it sounded obscene. They didn't leave for a long time and Blue swore from her room. She'd already been in bed for hours. Spider was scared of the sleepless morning ahead.

She finally came down alone in the living room, sitting at the window in the muddy orange light. The kids were already across the street on the basketball courts, out playing the first chance they got. It overcame her to remember the feeling of being an excited kid, waiting for the day to begin.

She'd forgotten it so completely.

16

They went out for breakfast to ease their post-Hallowe'en booze and candy hangovers. Blue congratulated herself on an excellent costume; she'd been a wizard and made Sally dress like a unicorn so she could ride on her back. She paid for breakfast since Spider was broke like usual. As they sat back with bellies full of Belgian waffles Spider recounted the nightmare she'd had the night before, waves of crabs scrabbling over an empty ocean bed of rocks. "We're gonna die sooner or later," she said. "And who the hell wants to live later?"

"Well," Blue said, "at least you have a sense of humour about it."

"We're stopping at the liquor store on the way home," Sally said, looking a bit green. "I need some hair of the wild dog." The rest of the afternoon passed by in the living room with a few slow beers.

Spider lit a joint at the window and watched the traffic. "All those people going nowhere," she said. "In a hurry."

It was unusually warm and tourists kept flooding the city like white bloated rats. It was sunny enough to still strip down and lie across the grass, smell barbecues three houses over. Blue had the only cigarette left so she and Spider each took puffs. At the park across the street some kids played on the basketball courts, and a couple of old drunks sat on the grass. The benches were empty.

Gerda phoned for a chat. When Blue hung up the receiver she told them her mother had a new boyfriend, a German composer named Holger. They made some dumb jokes about his name.

"We all have the day off," Spider said. She felt restless and bored. "Anyone up for the CC Saloon?"

"Holger horses!" Blue screamed.

"I don't see why not," Sally said. "Let's walk past the House of Cock. Bigfoot doesn't even know I'm back in town."

"Yeah, and we can find out if there's anything going on tonight," said Blue.

Spider got up, already feeling weird. She'd heard stories about the House of Cock. It was a big, filthy place full of boys. Frank lived there. She had driven over with Fergus a few times, but he never took her inside.

"What about Frank?"

"Fuck Frank," Blue said. "He's an asshole and everyone knows it."

The rest of her beer went down fast and Spider tried to loosen up. She sang a song to hide her nervousness. "Sally Pepper and baby Blue, the craziest drunks I ever kneeew...."

Bigfoot was a meathead who worked a construction job and sold weed on the side. Sally said he'd once owned a dog who'd ripped up the yard, completely. Spider and Blue had spent countless hours trying to figure out why Sally liked him. As they walked they discussed the rest of the boys at the House of Cock: Baxter, some kind of a cranky guitar god who slept all day like a vampire; Tobey, a good-natured punk drummer; and Frank, skidding through life on welfare. Once a month the guys in the house formed a band together and broke up because apparently Baxter was a legendary asshole and everyone disliked him.

"Maybe we should hit the liquor store first," Spider said on the other side of the park. She wasn't looking forward to seeing Frank.

"Zero to hero in three beers," Sally laughed and hit her shoulder.

"We should see what they already got," Blue said. "If we come with too much they'll think it's a party and drink it all. Those boys are beer pigs."

"They're *pig* pigs," Sally said then reconsidered. "But somehow nice. Except for Frank. He's such an asshole."

"Too bad he's so cute. What a waste."

"He always looks like he's up to something."

"Like how to get his nuts on your chin."

"Forget him," Sally said. "Chicks before dicks."

"Yeah," Blue said. "That's the motto!"

Spider felt destined to lose, and that meant anything could happen.

Rock music blasted through the windows at the House of Cock. A heap of old tires leaned precariously against the garage. Frank sat on the porch railing, picking at a guitar. A cute boy with brown hair jumped off the front steps and landed on his skateboard.

"Nice one, Otis!" Sally called.

"Ladies!" exclaimed Frank on the porch. "It's a fur posse!"

Sally said, "Is Bigfoot around?"

"Nope," Frank said. "Didn't you hear? Bigfoot went back to Winnipeg like a faggot. Otis moved in with his fruity pink blanket."

"How long is he gone for?"

"Who knows?" Frank looked over. "Hey Spider," he said, just short of sounding friendly. He wore sunglasses with silver frames and it was impossible to see his eyes. Someone had scrawled, 'The Best' across his T-shirt.

"Did your mom make that shirt for you?" she asked. Everybody laughed.

"Hel-LO!" Otis said, kicking his skateboard into his hand and coming over.

"Hey," Spider said. She looked at her feet.

Frank smirked. "Are you girls here to put out?"

"Can we have a beer first?"

"That's Frank for you," Blue said. "If we wait long enough he'll probably fall off the porch."

"He's a clown show," Sally agreed.

"Where you guys going?" Frank asked.

"To get beer."

"Good idea! How did you girls *know* I wanted some beer?"

"Come back and drink it here," Otis said. "With us." He looked at Spider and actually winked. She thought how she never got to meet boys like him. Then it occurred to her, in a sudden flash of paranoia, that his attention could be a big joke that Frank had concocted. He was that kind of an asshole.

Otis smiled and Spider saw his front tooth was chipped. It made him look scrappy. "I'll go get the beer for you," he offered. "What're you ladies drinking?" He smiled at Spider again. They gave Otis the money for two six-packs and he took off down the street on his skateboard. He kick-flipped off the curb, fell, and got up quickly.

"WIPEOUT!" Frank screeched. Otis jumped back on his board and kept riding.

They sat on the front steps while Frank played guitar. He sang a song about beer, then a song about a submarine full of lesbians. From the house a group of boys yelled and Sally looked through a window.

"They're playing video hockey," she said. "And it's so nice outside."

"It's the playoffs," Frank explained.

"Hey, you should have a barbecue," Blue said.

"Yeah!" Frank said. "I'll stick my wiener in your hot dog bun."

"Frank!" Sally said. "HAH HAH!"

"You shut up," Frank said.

Otis skated back up the walk. Spider couldn't believe anyone could carry that much beer on a skateboard. The cans were cold and he passed them out. Blue put the rest in the fridge. The boys yelled when she went in the house.

"Nice rack!"

"Heeeeeey, Blue."

Another screeched, "I've got blue balls!"

"What's up tonight?" Blue asked.

"What's UP?" a boy yelled. "How about my CACK UP yer ASS!" The room erupted in loud guffaws.

Blue slammed the screen door coming back outside. "Just walking through there made my IQ drop."

"And your tits grow," Frank added. They ignored him.

"This is a big house," Spider said.

"There's a garden," Otis said and jumped up. "Do you want to see the garden?"

Spider felt everyone look at her. "Okay," she said. She followed

dirtbags > 59

Otis around the side of the house. There was a large pile of dirt in the corner of the backyard.

"This is your garden?"

"Whaddya think I should plant?"

She circled the dirt and poked at it with a stick. "Purple bush beans," she said after a minute.

"Really?" Otis said. He leaned over. "You're cute," he said, "You've got little freckles on your nose." He sat down on the grass and gently pulled her arm. "C'mere," he said. "I'm gonna find you a four-leaf clover!" Spider knelt down beside him. Otis told her he'd found one a week ago.

They looked for a while and then he asked, "How do you know Frank?"

"I used to date his friend," Spider answered. "A long time ago."

"Who?"

"Do you know Fergus Finn?"

"Fergus? That motherfucker still owes me for an eight-ball!"

"Anyway," she said, "I know Frank. Everything he says is complete bullshit."

"Oh, that explains it."

Spider asked, "Explains what?" Otis shrugged and pulled her up.

When they came back around the side of the house she heard Blue say, "What's with Otis? I've never seen him get excited over anything except weed and a bag of potato chips." Spider felt her face redden and sat back down on the porch.

"You guys were gone for a while," Frank said. "Were ya humping in the garden? Garden humpers!"

"Shut up Frank or I'll drop you," Otis said. He sounded like he meant it. Frank shut up.

Otis gently took her hand. "Frank is twenty-two and a little underdeveloped for his age." Spider reached for another beer and Otis squeezed in beside her.

"I like your hair," he said. He ran his hand down its length on her back. "It's soft."

Her hair was getting long. Spider thought how sometimes when she was little Johnny brushed it out and she liked that most of all because he never made it hurt.

"Thanks," she said stiffly. "I grow it myself."

"Quit being a weirdo, Otis," Sally warned.

"Just because she's quiet it doesn't mean you can touch her," Blue said.

"What's this?" Frank said. "Women of the world unite?"

"That's right," Blue said, raising her fist. "Chicks before dicks!"

"I need a haircut," Sally informed them. "I hate this mop of mine." Frank began to sing a song he called 'Chickenhead.' Then he grabbed his crotch and started jerking like a spastic.

"If you can't control it we're leaving," Sally said.

Blue put her empty can on the railing. "We're leaving anyway. The beer's done."

"I'm going with Spider," Otis said. He took her hand again and this time she let him.

"Otis," Frank yelled. "We're gonna rehearse with Baxter at seven." Otis kept holding her hand. "Otis!" he yelled again. Nothing changed.

Sally finished her can of beer and threw it in the bushes. "There's going to be some trouble."

Blue laughed. "Starting tonight."

"You bitches are all the same," Frank said and went in the house.

dirtbags > 61

17

Otis invited them to see his roommate Baxter's band play a few nights later. Sally was too hung over to go out but Blue said she would meet her there. "You *can't* chicken out and stay home at the last minute."

"Otis is a doll," Sally told her. "You have to go."

Spider waited outside the bar. Blue said she'd be there after her shift at work though it could take her hours to show up. Spider considered going home then—she'd smoke a joint alone, watch TV, and fall asleep on the couch. It was such a depressing thought she took a deep breath and walked inside.

The bar was small and not crowded enough. Spider saw Frank right away, watching the door from across the room. One thing she knew about boys was that she could always catch them staring. Underneath those ball caps their eyes really moved around.

Frank stood with a bunch of guys. He said something when he saw her and they laughed loudly. It made her think of the jocks in the university cafeteria. She gave Frank a wide, fake smile then flipped him the finger.

Spider looked for Otis while trying to stand casually at the bar. He wasn't there and the beer couldn't go down her throat fast enough. She snuck the bottle out the back door to the parking lot where everyone went to smoke weed. There were only a few people standing around. A junkie jerked between them, asking for change. The music started up. Spider dreaded going back inside. She felt like an unsociable loser.

"You got any change? I just need bus fare," the man said. He held out a scabbed arm. "I need to get home to Seattle."

Someone behind her said, "Beat it, deadbeat!" The junkie

shuffled away. She turned around and there was Otis, giggling.

"Making friends?" he asked.

"Yeah. I've got personality."

"I saw you flash Frank the finger," he said. "You don't like him."

"He's garbage," Spider said.

"Well, *I'm* Otis."

They walked inside and he threw himself right into the pit. She stood on the side and watched Otis in his baggy pants and dirty shirt, thrashing to the band as the kids slammed wildly into each other. Every once in a while he stopped and bought her a beer before diving back in the pit. Spider watched Otis all night. He looked like he really knew how to have a good time. When the bar closed he put his arm around her waist. "I know where there's gonna be a party," he said. "Just a few blocks away."

Otis had a scar on his chin, five tattoos, and a smile like the sun. Blue showed up just as they were leaving. Everyone walked in a giant group from the bar like school kids on a field trip gone awry.

The party was in a basement with spray-painted wall murals of graffiti art and a couple of shabby couches to sit on. Small pockets of underage girls clustered together. Otis disappeared while Spider smoked with Tobey and his lilac-haired Chinese girlfriend. A skinny blonde boy in a dirty denim vest stood in the middle of the room shouting, "I'll fuck every slut in this place!"

When the liquor was gone Blue and Spider stole beers from the girls who didn't look legal and congratulated themselves. Otis pulled Spider onto his lap. Later one of the teenage girls puked on herself. Blue found her own ride home. Otis and Spider sat talking in the corner, doing line after line of his coke.

She kept feeling the rush. It was good stuff. They kept talking, and the conversation went on and on. They talked about many things yet always came back to more coke. "I don't do this much," she said.

"Me neither."

"You're doing a lot right now."

"Yeah," Otis said. "Just so I can talk to you."

The party began to wind down. Someone turned the lights on and off and the last few people watched the cockroaches scatter. Spider noted with glee that Frank was passed out on the floor.

Otis moved closer on the couch. He kissed her and she kissed him back. Her stomach rolled uneasily as she pulled away. "I have to go home."

"You just wanted my drugs," he said.

"That's not true," she said. "Well, I wanted to do your drugs, but I wanted to *talk* to you, too."

Otis walked her to the door. It was nearly morning. He asked Spider if he could call her later and when she said yes he kissed her again. Her head was full of coke and beer and useless feelings. Otis gave her money for the cab and she almost puked on the ride home while the nervous driver watched in the mirror.

The phone rang early that evening. It was Otis. "How bad is your hangover?"

"Medium to large," Spider groaned. "With a side of the skitters."

"Bum gravy?"

"Gross!"

"Let's have our hangovers together," Otis said. "Can I come by?"

Spider panicked. Her hair needed to be washed. She tried to recall if she had any clean underwear. Then she remembered how Otis had kissed her and decided it didn't matter. Unlike Fergus, he seemed really into her. Sally and Blue offered to stay over at Angelica's, as long as Spider promised to give them the details the next day. "With ALL the dirty words," Blue added.

Spider and Otis stayed up all night. Spider felt like she was seeing everything for the first time—the texture of the pillows, the light coming into the room. How the sky at five a.m. was a perfect cobalt blue.

The next day she and Otis sat on the couch, passing the bong. They'd fucked again as soon as they'd woken up. Spider was high and starting to feel a bit shy. Otis kept staring at her. Then he kissed her and all she could think about was his warm, wet mouth. "You're my girlfriend now," he said.

It was like that with Otis. He didn't have to ask.

When Sally and Blue got home they ran in and jumped on Spider as she lay on the couch. "So?" Blue squealed. "Did you get spread with his nutbutter?"

"Oh stop, you crazy romantic."

"I think you really like him," Sally said.

Spider put her head in her hands. "You're right," she said. "Something big happened last night."

"Nah," Blue said. "It was just his cock."

The day after sex with a boy the feelings never changed, and the big circles under Spider's eyes were the same. Her cunt ached a deep dull throb that still felt good, and during the day she thought back to all the dirty things they'd done the night before. Even three days later, remembering the way Otis had bit his lip made her stomach do a slow roll. All she could think about was sex with him again, and felt like some dull-witted beast.

18

Otis liked having a good time. He made fun of everything. One afternoon they got stoned in Stanley Park and he made fun of the trees. "Otis is a great guy," Sally said. "For one who parties all the time." She said he'd had a girlfriend once and when she moved away he'd worn dark glasses and stayed drunk for a month. Otis was cute and funny but the reason Spider liked him most was because he had a laugh that was insane and high-pitched. Otis actually giggled. He and Sally got along because she had a soft spot for anyone who was free with their weed.

When Otis woke up, he smoked a joint. Then another after breakfast. A few in the afternoon, one before and after dinner, three or four during the evening. Sometimes he woke up in the night to smoke weed just to go back to bed stoned. He liked video games, hockey, soft porn and drinking outdoors. He was moody and miserable when it rained and he couldn't skateboard. It seemed he knew every aging cocaine vulture in town and they had a shared history of good times. Spider had never seen him pass out or give anyone a rough time. Otis worked with Frank on a painting crew for an industrial-sized apartment complex. Their boss let them smoke weed on the job, and they could miss a day of work with an early morning phone call. Otis slept as late as he wanted, and never planned ahead.

One afternoon he told her that when he was seven his real mother had died of cancer. He'd never gotten over it. They sat on the back porch and he said, "I used to believe my mother was an angel." Otis hung his head sadly.

"I know what it feels like," Spider said. "To lose the only person in the world who accepts you for who you are." She put her arms around his neck. They spent the rest of the day smoking weed and kissing, for hours. Spider rode her bike home through strange neighbourhoods like she owned them.

Otis Renfrew. She even loved the sound of his name.

Sally and Blue were off work at ten and Spider had a plan to meet them downtown. She felt vulnerable walking down the street at night, because for the first time she couldn't stop smiling. In a corner grocery she bought a pack of cigarettes. The middle-aged clerk had a pleasant face and Spider burst out, "I'm in love!" He said nothing and gave back her change. The woman behind her applauded.

It was Retro night at Pandemonium, a giant dance club with overpriced drinks. The coat check girls were beautiful and vicious, with a mindless hostility bordering on assault. As Spider waited in line they sniped back and forth. One familiar-looking girl had short, stylish hair and Spider realized it was Kayla Sinclair, her one-time friend who had made middle school a misery. Spider watched her work the coat check. Kayla brayed to another girl about where to get knock off designer bags. Spider wondered if she ever talked about anything interesting. Kayla looked like she always had, beautiful and bored, only she wasn't as fresh anymore. It was as if she'd spent her whole life waiting to make an entrance, and time was running out. Spider thought of Otis, how that morning he'd kissed her and said, "You look even cuter than usual today!"

Instead of turning away Spider squared her shoulders. Sally had done up her hair and for the first time all night she was glad Blue had made her wear a low-cut, cherry red top. Spider knew she looked good.

At the front of the line Kayla looked at her for a moment and then gasped. "Omigod! Spider! How *are* you? You look amazing! Do you live here now?" Kayla reached her arms out toward her and Spider draped her jacket across them. Kayla stopped squealing. In fact, she stopped smiling all together. "Oh," she said, and handed her a number.

Spider slid a dollar across the counter. "Toodles," she said, wiggling her fingers. It was a classic Tara move she'd always found obnoxious. Back at the table she squeezed in beside Blue. "I went to junior high with one of those coat check girls," she said. "When I was thirteen she made my life hell."

"Which one is she?" Blue yelled. "I'll take a pin and pop one of those big fake tits!"

Spider looked at Kayla's pinched face as she scurried with an armload of coats. What she'd done had made her feel good, but only for a minute. She was struck with a sudden thought, that her brother used to have so much love for the world and somehow she had so little.

Sally paid for another round of gin and tonics. They sat at one of the huge circular tables and watched the hairdos and costumed club kids wiggle and squirm. "Let's go to the bathroom," Spider said. "I want to bust out this coke Otis gave me."

"Not me," Sally said. "No powders for a while. I never let my drug habits get out of control."

"It's funny that you've never felt that way about weed."

"Weed's not a drug. It's a flower. From the earth!"

"So is this," said Spider.

"Yeah? You've got uncut coke?"

Blue pulled her to the bathroom and they crammed together in a stall. "I wouldn't even *consider* being at an Eighties retro night without cocaine," she said. She sucked back her line with a giant snort. "That would *truly* be the end of irony."

"Well said."

"So how are things going with Otis, anyway? You randy bitch, you've been with him every night for two fucken weeks!"

"I'll tell you," Spider said. She took the bill and snorted her line, then began to rub her nose. "Well, actually, I don't know WHAT to tell you."

"Isn't that cute," Blue said. "You've got a big goofy smile on your face like you're wearing a sign that says 'Love just shit all over me.'"

"Nice talk," she said. "Another one?"

"Cut that shit little finer."

When Spider came home that night there were four messages from Otis.

"I love you more than liquor," he slurred. "I love you more than my next beer!"

Those were the sweet nothings she adored.

The House of Cock looked worse on the outside but the only real drawbacks Spider could see was that their bathroom never had toilet paper, and in the morning, no matter when she got up, there were always a couple of boys in the living room and she had to walk past them to get to the bathroom. Spider kept close to Otis on the couch, or stayed in bed and made him go to the kitchen for drinks. He didn't seem to care much about what the boys in the living room were doing. Frank generally ignored her.

The drugs became more obvious with his friends: Jango, Double-Barrel (known for his disgusting farts), and the diminutive

dirtbags > 69

Sparky, who was nineteen and looked forty-three. They seemed to accept her presence as an extension of Otis and soon going over to the House of Cock didn't make her uncomfortable at all. She found the conversations of boys familiar and pleasantly distracting.

"Pork's gross!"

"Shaddup!"

"You can eat it if it's kosher."

"What's that?"

"Dude, it's when they drain the blood outta..."

"You don't have a clue."

"He's an undercover Jew, waiting to expose how stupid we are."

"HAY! Which one of you clowns drank all duh fucken BEEHS?"

They went out for drinks. They did some lines. Spider thought they were doing just fine.

19

It was Blue's twenty-fifth birthday. Sally and Spider took her out for a birthday breakfast that slid into afternoon cocktails. They'd finished up some Chinese food before going to the CC Saloon. Blue had disgusting MSG farts. "It's my party," she sang. "And I'll fart if I want to!"

"I have to go meet up with Otis," Spider said, rising. "I'll be back soon." She had promised to lend him some money, which she didn't want to tell them.

Blue slammed her drink down on the table. "What do you mean? It's my goddamn birthday. ALL DAY!"

"I'll see you guys in a bit, I promise."

"It's your ass, Blue," Sally said. "You just drove her away."

"You're having separation anxiety," she accused as Spider put on her coat. "It's because you spend ALL your time with him."

"Look, I'll see you in an hour."

Blue flicked her wrist as if to get rid of a pest. "Whatever," she said and turned away.

Spider ended up in a rough bar sitting at the counter with a couple of guys she barely knew. Otis had asked her to wait while he left to buy some drugs and it was taking forever. The boy next to her called her a little macho bitch. She wore a short top and sat uncomfortably with a group of thugs, even though no one would fuck with her. A boy smiled from across the bar. Swinging off the stool she fell and tripped, then tried to do a little dance to cover it up. No one laughed, and when she glanced at the boy he was looking at a girl in the other direction.

Otis had taken the last of her money. Spider couldn't afford another drink and no one was buying. She didn't leave, even though she couldn't believe she'd ditched Sally and Blue.

Blue stopped wiping the counter and looked at Spider with an arched eyebrow when she crept in the kitchen the next morning.

"Thanks a lot," she said. "What, you can't be away from this guy for *one* goddamn night?"

"God, I'm so sorry." Spider felt terrible that she'd stood up Blue on her birthday.

Sally came into the kitchen yawning and opened the fridge. "Hey Spider," she said.

"It's only been six weeks and you practically live over there," Blue said. "Isn't this going kind of fast for a guy you barely even know?"

"What do you mean?" Sally interrupted. "It's Otis Renfrew."

dirtbags > 71

"So what?" Blue said. "I don't care if it's fucking Pete Moon!"

"She doesn't judge your boyfriends."

"I'm not stupid enough to really *fall* for a dirtbag."

Spider yanked a cupboard open. "No, you'd need feelings for that. Your instincts for self-preservation are too finely tuned."

"You *know* what I'm talking about."

"Whatever," Spider said. "I don't need to hear this."

Blue slammed down a pot then turned to Sally. "All I'm saying is what's so bad about Spider being on her own? Why is it so hard for her to be alone?"

"Who are *you* to say that?" Sally demanded. "Do you have something against happiness?"

"I don't have a problem with people being happy."

"Well, you're the only one complaining!"

Sally grabbed a soda and went back to her bedroom. She banged the door shut. Blue fumed and put on her earphones.

Spider walked slowly over to the House of Cock. All the way there she wanted to cry. Otis opened the door wide. "Thank you," she said.

She sat on the front steps of the House of Cock, complaining to Otis. Spider was even more broke than usual. At night she had begun to hear the shuddering of mice in the closet walls and thought it would drive her mad. Tobey banged on his drums downstairs, stopping now and again to swear loudly. "Just stay here," Otis said. "It'll be even cheaper rent."

"What about everyone else?"

"Who?" Otis laughed. "Those guys don't care."

Spider considered it. She'd spent every night there since the fight between her and Blue. The apartment seemed cold and tense. For over a year she'd lived with them and no one had ever exchanged a bad word. They didn't need her rent money anymore and it seemed pointless to stay in a place where she wasn't really wanted.

"What about you?"

"Baby, my shit is your shit," Otis said.

Slowly her stuff moved in.

20

The party never stopped at the House of Cock.

Every night the phone rang late. There were three a.m. calls for drugs, and a guy with a squeaky speed voice that kept coming over to try and sell bikes that were obviously stolen. Every time Spider came out of the bedroom with Otis a new crowd of people had arrived. Once it was an entire group of evil clowns who rolled around on the floor punching each other. Otis partied all night into morning, right through the next day.

Spider decided to make dinner one Friday night the first week she officially moved into the House of Cock. She had rarely seen anyone eat a decent meal and cooked a large pot of chili for the entire house. Otis looked at her suspiciously when she told him, as if he didn't believe food could be made in the kitchen. "That's earth food," Otis said when he lifted the lid. "I want space food!" He went to the phone and called his coke dealer. Tobey and Frank devoured the entire pot while she and Otis did a couple of lines on the coffee table. It didn't matter to Spider. She knew she wasn't much of a cook, anyway.

Blue called and asked Spider to meet her at work. She told the cook to make up some pasta even though the kitchen was closed. Blue had a way with her co-workers. The boy she had met while at the lodge had finished his tour in the bush and come to town to visit her. His name was Sid. He sat at a far table with his tanned skin and slight smile. After saying hello to Spider he sat back down in the corner. Spider could see why Blue liked him. He looked like any moment he expected Blue to leave him. Spider knew that feeling, loving someone even though you knew it would never be quite enough.

Blue's tiny fingers held a delicate wine glass. She seemed so tough yet Spider was always amazed at her thin wrist bones. "I'm sorry I was such a bitch about my birthday," she said. "Spider, you're like my little sister."

"I know."

"We miss you in the apartment. I worry about you."

"You don't have to, and I don't like it."

"It's just that—you can't just exist to prop these boys up."

Spider tried to think how she could explain it to Blue; the years of growing up in her family and the safeness she felt when Johnny was around. It didn't matter why her mother was angry, or what mean things the girls did in school. He was what she had on her side. Since he'd died it felt like a better life was simply gone without him. It was the background to where she expected to end up—breaking down alone, her heart unchained to anyone. And somehow, just with the easy way he moved in the world, Otis changed everything that mattered.

"He needs me," Spider said. "He says he gets into trouble when I'm not around."

"That's what I'm talking about."

"Everyone says things happen for a reason, but you know what, Blue? They don't. Life is just a bunch of meaningless, random events that only matter if they bring us pleasure or pain."

"Spider—"

"No, listen to me. When I'm with Otis I feel like something good is coming my way. And that...maybe I deserve it."

"Okay," Blue said finally. "I won't say another word."

Sid came over and put his arms around their shoulders. "You girls hangin' tough?"

"Always," they said.

Little by little Spider grew accustomed to her strange living space. She and Otis had a room upstairs, Baxter and Frank were on the first floor, and Tobey lived downstairs with his drum kit. It was easy not to care about home decorating. Everything was an ashtray to them: plants, mugs, pop cans, shot glasses, counter tops, floors. No one bothered to recycle or even take out the garbage until the stink was unbearable. The boys put up pictures of naked girls but agreed to confine their porn to one wall. They cooked giant slabs of meat on the kitchen counter grill and never went near a vegetable. Spider learned about the free cable hook-up, penalty shots and the universal remote. There was no denying their rapture with sporting events, Tuesday night fights, ass-facing passed out partiers, and, of course, tits and ass. Girls were a constant diverting conversation, a running lowbrow monologue to what they watched on television:

"Change the channel. Those guitar playing twins suck—"

"Big dicks!"

"Yeah, a fashion show! Let's see some *tits*!"

"Nice rack!"

"I'll bet she waxes her butt muff!"

They were amusing in their mindless sexism, and except for Frank she adored them.

Everything changed at night when Otis loved her. Spider felt herself opening like a sea flower until the fear took over, that her heart could not bear to be so full and she tried to love him less. When he slept she worried at her clumsiness, always in the dark, with that fear and his taste.

21

Frank found a girl. Not just any girl—a radiant nursing student named Candace. She was a bubbly club girl with a squeaky voice who loved to blast dance music. No one could figure out what the hell she was doing with Frank.

They met her one night when she and Frank stumbled in drunk at two a.m. Spider and Otis were curled on the couch watching some stupid movie on cable. Candace sat down on the floor and shared the last of her gin while they tried to explain the retarded plot of the film. She impressed Spider with her ability to jump into any conversation. Candace had springy blonde curls that made her seem perpetually giddy. After the movie was over a nature show came on. Candace was emphatic that her favourite monkey was the baboon.

She began to come by the house all the time. Spider liked watching Candace arrange her white nurse's uniform, hiding those crazy curls in a bun. In the mornings it killed her when Candace walked gracefully down the wobbly front steps of the House of Cock. She and Frank spent a lot of time laughing. He didn't seem like as much of an asshole anymore. Candace swept the floor and did the dishes. The house began to smell better. Sometimes Candace and Spider drank tea, relaxed and pleased in the clean kitchen, before the boys came home with their snorts and odours and noise.

The boys in the house played rough. If one of them passed out with their shoes on the other boys would slip a tab of acid into his mouth, or blow a straw full of coke up his nostril and watch him bolt off the couch. Otis made it clear Spider was off-limits since she was his girl. She had seen a lot of things she didn't want to from that position. Spider liked Candace but pretended not to notice the girls that still came in and out of Frank's room. She understood that what she saw in the house had to stay there. But sometimes she looked at Candace, at her innocence and enthusiasm that was so silly and sweet, and didn't want Frank to destroy that part of her. Finding out that he had been cheating on her was only a matter of time; scenarios were unfolding. It would break Candace's heart.

But it did seem that Frank tried to love her. He spoke to her gently, and accepted ridicule from the boys when he let her hang up plants in the house because she said they smoked too many cigarettes. He even watered them once or twice.

The boys liked to party and they liked cocaine. Spider began to know their codewords: gerbs, halfords, the Swiss bear. There was a little bump here, a little extra to stay up and keep the party going. Then more more more. Spider watched people, how the greediness always took over. They locked themselves in the bathroom in the middle of a party, huddled possessively in corners over their lines.

One night Spider came home and found Candace sitting alone on the couch, teary-eyed. "Everyone's upstairs in your room," she said. Her lower lip began to tremble. "I knocked and they wouldn't let me in."

"I'll be right back," Spider promised. She knew exactly what they were doing. Frank enjoyed keeping his drug use secret. Spider ordered them to let her in and the room full of boys looked at her. Otis stopped cutting mid-line.

"Candace is sitting downstairs alone," she hissed. "Don't be so fucking obvious."

"Thanks, baby," Otis winked.

Everyone came downstairs and the party resumed in the living room. Candace pulled her aside. "Thank you," she said happily. "You're such a good friend!"

Spider felt like a complete shit. "Please don't thank me," she said.

A few weeks later Frank got high and offered a rail to Candace. She had never done it before and refused to try. Spider was relieved and didn't try to understand her own hypocrisy. Candace warned them that the heart was a muscle, and if it beat too fast it could stretch out of shape and never work right again.

When Otis and Frank heard things like that it just made them get more out of control.

22

One night Otis didn't come home. He didn't even call. Spider lay in bed awake until morning, and thought how her life was about sudden disappearances. She imagined Otis sobbing at her funeral, how he would miss her if she were gone. These thoughts gave her comfort until she heard the front door opening and his shoes thump up the stairs.

Otis crawled in beside her. She rolled away. "You should have called," she said.

"Baby, it happens," he said. "I was partying at some guy's house and just got toooo high."

She didn't know if he was lying. The thought of Otis being with someone else made her feel sick and slightly insane. "Do you want to be with other girls?" Otis said nothing and looked at her. Spider sat up in bed, ready to shake him. "The least you could do is answer me!"

"Baby, you're number one," he promised. "I don't have eyes for anyone but you."

Otis had a way. Anything he said sounded true.

"Cheer up, buttercup," he sang in the kitchen when he woke up the next afternoon. Outside the rain fell in a fine mist. Spider stood staring out at the city, feeling dark and depressed. Otis stuck his head in the fridge and kept shaking his ass until she finally relented and laughed.

"I'm so crazy about you," she said. It was useless but good to feel that way.

"Well, I'm cuckoo over you!" he said. "CUUU-CKOOO!"

23

It was Christmas Eve at the House of Cock. Sally and Blue brought over a turkey and potatoes on their way to their traditional Christmas bender at the CC Saloon. The boys demolished everything. Spider realized how much she missed her friends and it made her feel sad and weird that she hadn't noticed before. Whenever Sally and Blue came to the House of Cock they didn't stay long. It seemed to Spider they couldn't believe she actually lived there.

Spider came out of the bathroom, rubbing her nose. She caught Blue watching her and tried to stop sniffling. Blue looked angry.

"What?"

Blue said nothing.

"What is it you want to say, Blue?" The coke had made her over-confident and antagonistic.

"Just this," Blue said. "Do you ever consider what your brother would think if he saw you now?"

It was a cruel thing to ask and they both knew it. Spider looked around. The kitchen floor always seemed dirty, even after it was washed. Marked furniture, peeling paint, porn taped to the walls, burnt utensils. "Yeah," Spider said, her eyes filling with tears. "He'd probably wish that my life was nicer."

A large mirror took up most of the coffee table. Otis dumped a pile of coke on it in front of him. Spider didn't feel like doing lines all night, being runny-nosed and talkative in a room full of people she didn't know. Sally and Blue were long gone. Tobey was at his girlfriend's house and Candace was spending Christmas in

Kamloops with her parents. Spider hung out in Baxter's room for a while. He was an okay guy if you agreed with everything he said. The people in Baxter's room were smoking a speed pipe. She'd found out when she moved in why he was so bad-tempered and had odd sleeping patterns. He asked if she wanted some, too.

They called it riding the snake. The skinny glass pipe looked dangerous and the smell was like burning plastic. The first time Spider didn't like the smoke, it made her jittery and buzzed and the room got hotter. "Gimme more heat," someone said, grabbing the pipe. Then Spider couldn't wait to do it again.

Otis sat at the kitchen table with a group of people smoking a joint and she crept up beside him. "No new joiners!" he bellowed, then turned and saw it was Spider. "Except for you," he smiled.

The speed made her feel high yet strangely sober, like she could party all night. Otis could tell she'd been in Baxter's room. "Be careful," he said. "Some of those people would strangle you for the frost in the pipe."

Two rough-looking men in dirty coats began to yell at each other. It was the downward slide of the party when the black hole began to open and the drugs were running low. Otis pulled out a guitar and began to strum. Everyone in the room quieted down.

Spider realized then why she loved him. Otis made everything seem like it was going to be okay for a little while longer.

The next morning was Christmas day. They didn't have presents or a tree. Otis handed her a small sealed bag of shiny crystal shards. His gift was a bag of speed. "It's a white Christmas," he said. He and Spider snorted a huge line of crystal meth, then another. Her nose felt like a burning spike had been shoved up to her brain. Otis turned up the volume and they lay down on the couch to watch cartoons. All at once the screen doubled and she felt red and warm, hot and cold. A thin film of strange-smelling sweat covered her skin. The room folded in half.

Spider closed her eyes. She was riding the snake and felt the pulsing red scales. The snake was in front of her, beating through her body, becoming the colours behind her eyelids. She rode it through the universe then back into her veins. Her body seemed a perfect machine. It was so much at once she just breathed.

She heard a voice say, "You speeding up, Spider?"

The music thumped through the walls into the soles of her feet. Otis led her up to bed and time stretched out to infinity. They took off each other's clothes quickly. Spider jacked him off hard and then the snake was a long skinny cock getting hotter. His hair became coarse and black, oily and thick like the hair of a beast. She felt the roughness of his body and every punishment it had taken. There were flashes in her brain of their baby in a sonogram, growing weird and misshapen in her belly. His cock was like a giant nerve going all the way through her. Spider's heart turned over and over.

They stayed in that state for days. Crazed.

Speed.

Her body could take demands for only so long. One morning Spider dropped and fell asleep for an entire day. When she woke up and looked in the mirror she saw broken veins, deep black and purple shadows beneath her eyes. Three scabs on her cheek that looked like small holes. She hadn't eaten for days and it terrified her that the body could break down so quickly. The muscles in her back and side felt twisted and hard. She could barely move her neck from side to side.

She knew that this life would kill her. It wouldn't even take that long.

Standing at the mirror that morning, with the sun coming through the cracked window like a virus, Spider saw her end. And didn't want it. She thought, *The snake has black black eyes.*

24

On Easter Sunday Candace broke up with Frank. She'd found a condom in the garbage can and a crumpled phone number. She refused to talk while she packed up her things. No one knew if she'd found out about all the other girls or just one. Spider wondered if a better friend than she had told her, or if Candace had figured it out for herself. But she left Frank quietly, and that seemed to surprise him the most. It was a hard lesson to learn about boys like that. They only respected the girls that dumped them.

Frank wasn't the same after Candace left. There were always girls calling for him, a steady stream of young, half-naked girls coming out of his room, but he didn't seem happy about it. Spider knew he'd never understand why.

25

Spider had been dragging her ass at work, fighting a cold, when Ralph sent her home after she'd snapped at a customer who'd asked her, "Are the books in order by author or title?" As soon as she walked inside the House of Cock she smelled something strange. Otis and Frank were not at work, and sat on the floor of the living room playing video games, eyes glassy and glazed. Spider saw two pipes. They'd been smoking crack. Otis was blasted.

Otis jumped up and held the pipe out in his hand. He looked sweaty and nervous. "I'll throw it away," he said. "Just say the word."

The only thing Spider knew for sure about Otis was that he never did what anyone told him to do. And if he was stoned she wanted to be as high as he was, too.

She shrugged. "Is there some for me?"

Otis sat back down. Frank laughed and picked through the ashtray.

Spider watched Otis get high. He aged right in front of her, swirling the smoke in his mouth before he exhaled, mouth trembling. Then there was nothing on his face, just his slack lips and tongue. She thought how he didn't seem like her boyfriend anymore, but an empty *thing* sitting next to her on the couch, putting his hot, claw-like hand on her leg. It made her feel so hopeless and dirty she held the smoke in her lungs and shut the world away.

In the morning she felt as though her joints had been replaced with bits of broken glass. Her cunt was sore because after Otis smoked crack he wanted to fuck. He was like some kind of horny zombie with a self-lit furnace and after awhile that feeling of disgust actually started to turn her on.

When Spider went back over it later, how Otis told her he'd throw away his pipe if she said the word, she thought he might have said, "please."

She tried it once, twice, three times, four. The oily taste in her mouth she began to crave as soon as it was gone. It coated her tongue, seeped through her skin, heated up the world with a dull red glow. Spider found out all right. The smell of burnt powders and ash in an empty pop can she recognized right away. And every time she smelled it she wanted it again.

She hadn't even known Otis did dingers before he left for work. That sometimes he came home and did them at lunch. Soon Spider began to dread the grim look on his face as he searched for the packet he hid in the bedroom. He'd sit with a spoon and lighter, cooking up coke and baking soda to smoke with cigarette ash in his pipe. Then he wouldn't do anything else for the rest of the night.

Spider called Blue to borrow some money. They circled the block then met Blue in the park across from her building. Blue and Otis kept squabbling. "You live in a house with broken boards," Blue said to him. "And why is no one ever allowed in the garage?" The cops seemed to be everywhere.

They went to the liquor store then back to the park. Blue told an involved story of stealing an ice cream truck and getting stuck in a sand dune. Spider was captivated. When Blue smiled it changed the bones on her face.

"TRUE LOVE RULES!" Otis carved on a bench with his pocketknife.

Blue talked about Sid, her favourite boyfriend, who'd left for the forest with a tree planting crew and would be gone all spring and summer. Spider thought it would be hard to lose someone and still have them so close. But then she looked at Otis.

26

Dandelions were growing beneath the broken canoe by the side of the house. A long-bearded man in a heavy coat walked past muttering, bare yellow feet on the pavement. Spider smoked on the porch and looked at the sky. The clouds moved past like buses.

Inside, the party was getting out of control.

The coke wasn't very good. "Diesel fuel," she said, when Otis cut her another line. It was going to be a bad one: nose plugged, ears stuffed, a headache cutting across her forehead. Frank cornered her by the fridge, high and squawking like a bird. He was so skinny she could see his shoulder bones poke his shirt. "SQUAWWWWK! SQUAWWWK!" His throat moved thickly. It was a horrible sound. He came closer and closer until she was about to scream then suddenly stopped.

Spider escaped to the back porch for some air. A couple was making out on the filthy couch amid rat droppings. Spider could see the end of the party ahead—sweating and hopeless, wanting sleep so badly it ripped her mind apart.

Everything in the house seemed to be rotting; there was mold under the sink and Otis had a broken tooth. The front steps were busted. The fridge door opened and closed as people took out more beers. The sound of another tab popped was like snapping wood in a log hold where Spider sat precariously on top.

Otis was smoking crack when she came into the living room. He was jittery, his lips slightly white.

"Whoooa," he said, passing the pipe. "I just about saw the sun that time."

Some sketchy-looking guys smoked in the corner. A skinny

girl had passed out on the chair with her legs spread. The music was loud and furious. For the first time, being at the House of Cock didn't seem safe.

Spider tried to make herself small beside Otis on the couch. He kept twitching, jumping up and down to smoke the pipe. When he squeezed her leg his hand felt like meat going through the motions and no warmth passed between them.

"I saw Candace last week," some guy said. "Dude, she's hot. Mind if I fuck her?"

"Go ahead," Frank said. "I don't care if you shit in my pond."

Spider missed Candace. They had survived benders and breakdowns and the cycle of poverty for these vultures, people scavenging for cigarettes and unfinished drinks. Frank spat on his own kitchen floor.

She went upstairs to her bedroom and locked the door. For hours she watched shadow dragons fight on the walls. Two white pills put her to sleep. When she woke up it was early morning. The house was thankfully quiet when she went downstairs to the kitchen for water. Some people talked with low voices in the living room. Spider peeked around the corner. Frank and a few guys sprawled around the room.

The skinny girl was passed out on the couch. Someone had pulled down her jeans.

"Take off her fucking panties, man."

"Diddle 'er," someone else said.

Spider froze, terrified. The voices dropped lower. She thought what those boys in high school had done to her best friend Jenny White, how she herself had been a young, drunk girl upstairs at a party so long ago. Spider clenched her fists and marched into the living room.

"EVERYONE get the FUCK out," she hollered. "NOOOOW!"

The girl on the couch woke up and looked around, confused.

Except for Frank, the boys stumbled out the front door. Spider called a cab for the girl then crept back to bed, curling into the tightest ball she could. Otis hadn't been in that room, but it didn't matter. She wanted nothing to do with the people they'd become.

27

Spider told Blue everything. They sat quietly at the counter in the bar.

The stools wobbled and Blue draped her cold arm across Spider's back. Spider knew it had to end with Otis, who was nothing like the person she'd met. Now all she saw was the tail-end of a once-charming boy on his way down a long, ugly slide.

When Otis was high he told the same stories: of being cheated and robberies and war. A cold rain hitting the windows made him anxious, he felt a menace outside like a rumble. Last night he'd told her, *the Devil is on me.* And he'd known it for years.

Otis had addictions: crack, alcohol, lines of cocaine. His face had begun to waste away to a giant, sucking jaw and he started to have the look of addicts. They tried to smile but were baring their teeth.

The weight of Spider's anger had gone but an impression remained. Her limbs were tired and heavy. "Something's different now," she told Blue. "I can't sleep anymore. Otis keeps falling down." He fell into the bathtub, down the back stairs. He did the funky chicken all across the floor.

"He'll be dead by the time he's twenty-four," Blue said. She held up her tiny, rough hands. "Spider, you have to stop loving that boy."

When Spider got home Otis was passed out on the couch. She waited for him to wake up, smoked cigarette after disgusting cigarette. Even after a shower she felt dirty. Otis hadn't gone out on any painting jobs for weeks. Tobey took his drums and split just when rent was coming due. Baxter spent all his time at his new girlfriend's. The house was filthy, there was no food, and no one would lend them any more money. They'd already returned all the bottles. Spider felt shame to be out in the sun.

"Baby, we need cigarettes," Otis whined. She ignored him because he hated that. He complained to Frank that Spider didn't love him anymore. She didn't hear what Frank said back. Then Otis took his stereo to the pawnshop and came back with a huge grin on his face that she recognized right away.

The only thing funny anymore was that everything he did annoyed her.

Frank ran down to the corner to meet his dealer, and when he came back Otis got out his cooking spoon. It was a beautiful morning and already Spider felt defeated by the day and the sticky smell of crack, oily and sweet. She started to clean up and when she dumped the ashtray Otis yelled.

"What the fuck ARE YOU DOING?"

Otis had never shouted at her before. Spider went up to the bedroom. Her hands shook as she shoved a few things into a duffel bag and dragged it across the room. Her heart was as heavy as the mattress on the floor.

Otis watched her walk across the living room. At the front door she said, "Otis, I can't live like this."

He picked up the pipe. And blazed.

Sally and Blue tried to take her out for a good time, but when people talked all Spider could do was watch their mouths moving. She stared at the ceiling and jumped whenever the phone rang. Otis stayed in her head like a record that kept going around and around that awful first moment when she realized he didn't love her anymore. She felt a lingering sense of disbelief they had once been so happy.

The girls went to the Quarry for drinks. Spider stayed in. The phone rang late but she didn't answer. She was too afraid it was Otis and had no idea what to say. That night she dreamed of him, that his eyes melted the ice between her bones. In the morning Spider woke up and felt her heart racing. Maybe it did matter to Otis that she loved him after all.

No one answered when she called the House of Cock. Blue and Sally just shook their heads. It had only been three days. "I have to see him," Spider said. Blue started to say something and Sally stopped her. They knew the story. There wasn't much of a goodbye.

Spider tapped her feet the whole bus ride home, jumped off on the corner and ran down the street. As she climbed the front steps she knew then how much she loved Otis, even his excesses.

She wanted to get high.

Spider opened the front door. Frank sprawled on the couch. His face was grey and his whitish lips were covered with ash. A dirty blanket nailed over the window made the living room even darker. The house was much too quiet. Spider had a horrible feeling that she'd stayed away too long.

"Where's Otis?"

Frank looked at her. His lips were so dry he could barely move them. Something was wrong. She looked upstairs and in the kitchen. Then she checked the bathroom. The door was opened a crack and she saw his blue-printed shirt. "Otis? What are you *doing*?" Spider knocked but he didn't answer.

"Fucking cunt," Frank croaked from the couch. "Won't get out."

"Otis?"

Spider pushed the door open. And then she saw him.

Everything was blue. The shower curtain, his shirt, even the light coming through the window. His hands and face were blue, like the body paint he'd used for zombie make-up on Hallowe'en. But that wasn't what made Spider think he was dead. It was the look of fear and surprise on his face.

She screamed and the sound of the scream scared her and made her scream even louder. Electric shocks went off throughout her body. She ran into the living room and dialed 911. She couldn't stop her limbs from jerking. Frank didn't move.

Spider ran back to the bathroom and pulled Otis off the toilet. He landed on the floor with a sick, heavy thud. She pressed her ear against his chest but there was too much sound in her head to hear. Her fists beat on his heart over and over. His eyes began to twitch.

"FRANK!" she screamed. "HELP ME!"

When the ambulance blared in the distance Frank bolted out the back door. "Fucking cops are going to come!" he shouted. "Look at all the drugs!"

The paramedics were there in minutes. Otis took shallow breaths, his face now a greyish-blue. They were quick and efficient, placing him on a stretcher with an oxygen mask and rolling him right out. One of them wore too much aftershave.

A neighbour gave her a ride to the hospital. Spider sat in the emergency room of Vancouver General on a hard orange chair. A woman on a stretcher moaned, her mouth frozen grotesquely to one side. A well-dressed man sobbed in the corner. It all came over Spider again: falling through space and Johnny's crushed legs. The smell in the hospital was the same as the night her mother had woken her up to say that Johnny was dead.

Spider waited and knew nothing would be okay between her and Otis ever again.

An hour later, a doctor came. The suited man in the corner now wept into a handkerchief. The doctor put his cool hand on her arm. "Otis has suffered a fairly mild heart attack," he said. He was a tall, Asian man. His face looked genuine and kind.

"What?"

"Miss Mackenzie," the doctor said. "Otis is twenty-three years old with no major health problems. His heart should be a strong muscle. One reason for cardiac arrest in someone so young is chronic drug use. Okay? And now there are certain risks for Otis that will be unavoidable."

"But he's all right?"

"Otis needs medication and rest, but most of all he has to make some serious lifestyle changes," the doctor said. "If he ends up back here again it's going to be a lot worse. It will most likely be fatal. You understand?"

"Yes," Spider said. "I do."

A police officer came to the waiting room to take her statement. The officer was an unsmiling blonde who wore her hair pulled back so tightly it stretched the skin on her face. She interviewed Spider on the hard plastic chairs in the waiting area and wrote the answers down in a tiny black notebook. Spider said

Otis was her ex-boyfriend and she hadn't seen him in awhile. Her ID still showed Blue and Sally's address. She said she didn't know any of the other occupants of the house. That the door had been open. She'd found Otis inside alone.

Otis lay on the hospital bed sleeping, his skin a slight greenish colour. There was an IV running into his hand and an oxygen tube in his nose. Spider stood there for a long time and then pulled the curtain closed again.

The streets were getting dark. As Spider walked away from the hospital she thought how Otis didn't know she used to rub his head when he slept, just so he would have nice dreams. It was late by the time she got to Sally and Blue's. The rain had completely drenched her and Spider was very cold. Sally Pepper opened the door. "What's wrong?" she said, the moment she saw her face. "Spider, what happened?"

Spider shivered all the way into the living room. "Otis had a heart attack." It sounded so absurd to say out loud she began to giggle.

"Oh my god."

"Oh, he's okay. It's just funny. I mean he's not even twenty-four." She had to lie down on the couch she was laughing so hard. Then Spider began to cry and it was hard to tell the difference. The thought of how much she would miss Otis seemed sick and hopelessly sweet, like the strawberry milkshakes he made when they were coming down hard.

They wrapped Spider in a quilt and put her in Blue's room to sleep. Sally made her take a Valium with a mug of orange juice.

Spider lay stiffly on the bed. Darkness covered her like a blanket. She tried to block out the pictures in her head of Otis on the bathroom floor, blue face and cold skin. She thought of him dying alone in the bathroom, how it all could have happened so differently. When sleep finally came it hit her like a fist.

28

Spider picked up the phone. "Dad?" she said. "It's me. I want to come for a visit. I need some money to get home. Can you help me?"

Things had changed. "Talk to your mother," he said.

"Whatever you need," her mother said.

Spider looked out the window at the endless cars, semis rumbling, motorcycles like single blades down the middle of the highway. The traffic started and stopped like a small army. The bus drove away from the city and with it the boys she had loved there; that long, sweet September with Fergus; Otis' wild laughter, and how they had made such a strange home for a while.

A woman began to sing Janis Joplin at the back of the bus. When Spider heard "Summertime" it made her feel sad and overwhelmed. After everything that had happened between her and Otis she would become just another person he used to know. It was a long ride, and it all mixed and swirled together in Spider's head, washed away like watercolours. She thought of the strange attachments the dead have with the living. Johnny was on her mind.

The bus depots beckoned her home that warm October night.

PART TWO:

A Hard Light

29

Spider had never been what anyone would call a happy girl.

It was a small town in the mountains, surrounded by forest. The men cut up the trees that were sent to the sawmill. Most of the fathers in town worked there, or at the pulp mill that blew out yellow smoke which turned the hills and riverbanks orange. It was a hard town, ugly and cold. In the winter people got lost and froze in the snow. There were avalanches and black ice, dangerous curves on the mountain roads. Winter lasted half the year. Survival meant the economy of movement.

Spider's mother had photo albums of herself, in bathing suits and short dresses. They were labeled "Before." The pictures of her later on as she grew bigger with Johnny, then Spider, were labeled "After." She had met her husband in a local diner and soon dropped out of secretarial school. Spider's father had once been a handsome man. He had a very short temper. When he wasn't at work he watched TV, went hunting, and fished on weekends. Sometimes he sat on the porch and drank beer. He had dismantled bombs in the war. Long, thin scars covered his stomach and back. He wore heavy shirts in July. He never complained about the cold.

Johnny had just turned three when his mother explained that his baby sister was growing inside her swollen belly. "No!" he screamed. "Take it back!" He was so against this addition to the family that his parents allowed him to pick out his new sister's name. Already Spider's mother was afraid of her children. Johnny had decided on the name Bambi, after his favourite movie, until the day he stood in the hospital room and saw the tiny red baby wrapped in a white blanket with the fine black hairs on her head.

"Spider," Johnny said.

At first Spider's mother refused, but they'd made a promise. Spider's father never went back on his word. It was the last argument he ever won against her.

30

They lived in a house with a yard and rhubarb growing wild. A knotted white rope on a tree branch and a blue plastic pool. Her brother snuck down to the river to play and made Spider stay in the yard. The lilac bushes were her big purple friends. She ran barefoot up and down the lawn. There was a cat that lived next door named Smokey Joe. Then they moved into a duplex, and then another, each one with a smaller yard until there wasn't one at all.

Spider's mother tried to cuddle her daughter and put curls in her hair. Spider hated being confined under blankets and early on had the feeling of wanting to get away. She was not an affectionate child. Her mother went into the hospital and had her tubes tied; her father had a vasectomy. They did not want any more children.

Johnny and Spider had to play quietly because their father worked the night shift at the sawmill and slept during the day. Sometimes their laughter woke him up and he rose from the bedroom with the belt like a great, dark shadow. They never told their parents on each other. It was the first code of honour that their tiny hearts followed.

31

Johnny loved machines. Things came apart and back together easily in his hands. He'd play with motors, wheels, engines, anything that moved. Johnny hid out whole afternoons alone taking apart his toys. Spider spent most of her time trying to find him. If he were in the right mood he'd answer her questions as long as they weren't too dumb. Mostly she waited until he had time for her. "You're just a little spider," he'd say. "I could crush you with my foot!"

Johnny built snow forts and bike jumps. Sometimes he took Spider with him when he played in the neighbourhood with his friends. She sat on the sidewalk and watched their games, got to chase the runaway balls. They played soccer and stickball and street hockey. It was outlawed to cry in front of them.

Spider had gold-brown eyes and black hair and smashed bugs on the sidewalk. She liked to see guts.

A week before Spider started kindergarten her mother gave her a perm that smelled bad and burned her head. Spider screamed and Johnny ran to the bathroom. He stood by sadly while she cried.

Finally the day came. Spider walked proudly with her brother to school. They had the same new sneakers, blue with yellow stripes. Johnny took Spider to her classroom and pushed her inside. Her kindergarten teacher was Ms. Dixon. Ms. Dixon had curled blonde hair and wore so much mascara her eyelashes looked like tiny spears. Right away Spider loved the shiny paper and felt pens and coloured squares on the floor to sit on. They had their very own hook in the coat room, which smelled like apple juice and pee. Spider tried hard to colour inside the lines. She wanted red checks and gold stars so she could be as smart as her brother.

32

Sometimes Spider's parents drove over to the next town to play cards with Uncle Nick and Auntie Marlene until Auntie Marlene got sick with a tumour in her brain and died. But before the headaches she wore flowered shirts with no sleeves and smoked long cigarettes with her wrist bent to one side.

The adults sat around the kitchen table playing Canasta and drinking. Auntie Marlene's fingernails were yellow and thick and she drank her special drinks then made sounds like a bird. Spider stood beside her while they played cards, and lined up the butts with the matches she'd used in the ashtray. "Go wash your hands," her mother ordered. Uncle Nick threw down some cards and cursed. Spider found his moustache terribly handsome. He always held the matches for her to blow out after he'd lit his cigarettes, and had once let Spider draw curly hairs all over his fake leg with her brown crayon.

Johnny was upstairs in their cousin Bobby's room. Bobby was

already a teenager. He had long hair and pimples and Spider had never seen him smile. She crept upstairs and peeked around the corner. There were pictures of topless girls with their tongues out on the walls of his room. Bobby saw her and kicked the door closed with his foot.

Spider went back downstairs to the living room and watched television, a show about Sea World, and she rolled around and around the floor like a seal. Underneath the couch she saw a pile of magazines and pulled one out. There were pictures of naked women and hairy men touching each other. She turned the pages with gusto.

Spider's mother loomed over her. "Give me that," she ordered, and tore the magazine from Spider's hands. "My god," said her mother, looking at the picture. "What filth," she said and looked at another. She jerked Spider up off the floor and pushed her down the hallway.

"I KNEW this one had been quiet for too long," her mother crowed. She was flushed with drunk excitement as she told everyone in the kitchen what she'd caught Spider doing. They all laughed except Auntie Marlene, who gave her mother a strange look. The boys came downstairs and Spider's mother told them too, imitating Spider's expression when she'd been caught with the magazine. Spider closed her eyes and began to freeze, and when the boys started laughing she was frozen all the way through and didn't hear anything, at all.

Spider's parents lived, debt-ridden, on the edge of middle-class neighbourhoods with other people like them. Everyone wanted more than they had.

Finally her family moved again, into one of the few houses on the outside of a trailer park. Some of the kids said, "This is a

TRAILER park, not a HOUSE park." Johnny chased them out when they tried to come into their yard.

Spider usually walked home with Danny and Paul. Their neighbourhood was farther away from school than any other, except for the kids who took the bus. Danny had white blonde hair and wore shoes so old they had to be taped up. Paul was a short kid with freckles and a brown bowl cut. They walked together because they were all scared of the bullies in Grade 5. Danny kept getting beaten up by his semi-retarded brother, Ben.

It was springtime and they walked the long stretch of highway, past the arena on the edge of town, up and down a large hill. The day was warm and Spider tied her jacket around her waist. The sun made the part in her hair feel hot.

They were almost home when Amy Flowers rode past then stopped. "Hi Spider," she said. "Do you want to ride my bike?"

Amy Flowers was one of the prettiest girls in Spider's third grade class, and she lived in a house at the trailer park, too. She had wavy brown hair and a shiny red bike that made Spider's stomach hurt every time she saw it.

Danny picked up an old shoelace lying in the dirt and whipped her silver fender. Amy screamed. Her over-reaction startled Spider. Amy tried to ride away but her feet got caught in the pedals. Paul hit her tire with a stick and Amy screamed again, louder. At first Spider was afraid but Amy sounded so stupid she laughed.

That winter Danny and Paul threw Spider into a snow bank and made her open her jacket and unbutton her shirt. They poked her chest and told her she'd never have boobs. Paul rubbed her face in the snow.

Spider rolled over and stayed there for a long time after they left.

At home her mother yelled at her for being late. The next day at recess Spider put a rock in a snowball and threw it at Amy Flowers' head.

33

Their father got a promotion at the sawmill. It made her mother happy because now they would have more money and she could keep up with her ugly sisters. Their father had never been home much and when he started on the day shift as a floor manager they saw him even less. On the weekends her parents went to visit Uncle Nick. Johnny said he had become an alcoholic after Auntie Marlene died and that's why they weren't allowed to see him. Cousin Bobby had quit school and lived in the basement with his girlfriend, Rhonda. Spider had met her once, after the funeral. She had crooked front teeth and the same angry look on her face as Bobby.

Johnny filled Spider's empty hours. He took her to the corner store when they got their allowance. They bought pop and chips then dropped candy bars and gum down their pants into their underwear, sometimes shoved comic books up their shirts. The owner was a fat guy with white hair who didn't seem to like kids much. At home they'd go down to Johnny's room in the basement and spread out the loot like robbers after a big heist. He taught Spider how to play backgammon and poker and chess. Johnny and Spider had a secret spy hole under the back porch, and set traps for kids that tried to steal their bikes. They spit on their palms and shook with a secret handshake.

Spider loved Johnny more than anyone else in the world.

34

The least popular girl in Spider's class was April, a scrawny, bruised girl who wore thick eyeglasses in huge, pink frames. Her mother delivered the town newspaper and the story went that her parents were hippies and April had been born in a tree house. One of April's eyes was crossed and magnified behind her glasses. Sometimes when the girls were skipping at recess they let her have a turn. Every time she did they dropped the rope and every time April kept on jumping.

But it was the same with Spider. The girls in school did not like her. They moved their desks away and there were big gaps around her whenever the class stood in line. Every one laughed if she missed the ball in gym. Spider's worst fear was that her brother would find this out. At night she prayed for fourth grade to be over.

Spider devised a system. She got to school late and spent noon hour in the library. Her favourite books were about vampires and witches and magic spells. She tried to take inventory of good things about herself: Her fingers were small and good at untying knots. She could run pretty fast. Her brother liked her, most of the time. That was about all she came up with.

Spider only tried once to fake a sickness so she could stay home. When her mother came into Spider's room in the morning she pulled up the blankets and said, "I'm sick."

Her mother raised a suspicious eyebrow, as if her inner radar would have sensed an oncoming illness must sooner. "You don't look sick," she said. She took Spider's temperature. "You don't have a fever," she said. "Get up."

Spider pretended to faint on the bed, right back on top of the folded blankets. Her mother said, "Enough!" Still Spider did not move. Her mother carried her to the bathroom and dropped her in a warm bath. Spider clung limply to the side of the tub. "My stomach hurts," she whimpered. "There's ringing in my ears." Johnny had recommended that one. Her mother called for an appointment and they drove to the doctor's office.

The doctor had blonde hair and bad skin. He was a nice man. When Spider told him her symptoms he said she would have to get some tests done and he might have to take pictures of her brain. It was pretty exciting for a Tuesday afternoon.

"She was *perfectly* fine last night," Spider's mother protested. Spider could tell the doctor didn't like her mother very much and she stuck out her tongue a bit to the side, trying to look as sick as possible. Spider wanted to stay in a hospital forever, in a white world with her own mini-TV and different flavoured Jell-O, everyday.

"Now, which ear had the ringing again?" the doctor asked.

"Right," Spider said.

"You said it was the left one," her mother said.

"Right," she said. "The left."

The doctor looked at her mother and then they left the room to talk. When the doctor returned he said to come back in a few days if she had the same symptoms. Spider knew she was in for trouble by the look on her mother's face.

Johnny stayed out in the garage while their father spanked Spider with the belt. Spider knew he could hear anyway, along with the rest of the shitty neighbourhood: the guy the next row over who killed cats, and Amy Flowers, four houses down. Afterwards Spider went to the backyard and watched Johnny and his friend Tucker take apart an old lawnmower. She bent her head low and tried not to sniffle.

"You can't fool them that easy," Johnny said. "Ringing in the ears *and* blurry vision. That's what you say. Or else they'll think you're a hypochondriac."

"Don't call me names!"

"Spider, relax."

"I hate it here," she said. "I'm gonna run away!"

"Don't be so stupid," Johnny said. "You'd make it as far as the baseball diamond."

"Hey, why don't you go down there now and wait for a game," Tucker said.

"One should be starting in about two months," Johnny said.

They laughed loudly. Spider shut her eyes and let the tears slide. "Jesus Spider, we're just kidding," Johnny said, embarrassed. "What's *wrong* with you?"

The boys said she could come with them and they rode their bikes down to the edge of the park. At the end were trees and a little creek, and after that the forest started. Sometimes bears came out to eat garbage, and there were cougars and coyotes in there, too. Spider's fear of wild animals was nothing compared to her fear of the unknown in sixth grade, or that the girls in junior high would be even meaner than the girls in elementary school, and more of them.

Johnny let her have a drag of his cigarette. The smoke tasted oily and strong. Little pieces of tobacco stuck to the end of her tongue and she spat them out. Her throat hurt and her tongue burned. It felt good.

35

Spider's new school was concrete and huge. All the elementary schools came with their own reputation: Crown Heights and St. Joseph's (rich), Mission Flats (rowdy) and Spider's school, Birchmont (hick). The only school worse than hers was Diefenbaker, which had a patch of concrete instead of a field. The kids from Diefenbaker were bigger and had all grown up downtown.

The first thing Spider noticed was the two rows of double-thick metal fencing that surrounded the school like a prison. Everything inside was bolted down. Kids got bussed in from all over the mountain and in the mornings the hallways were frenzied like a shark feeding. The girls wore make-up and curled their hair in the bathroom mirrors with butane irons. They wore tight jeans and short shirts, big earrings and high heels. Spider's favourite shirts said, "Beach Bum" and "I Wanna Be a Trucker!" The older girls in school looked like pretty, shiny dolls. Spider once had a Wonder Woman Barbie, and when Johnny sandpapered off the boobs she'd become so hysterical she was never allowed to have another. Girls generally scared and confused her. Spider felt like there were rules no one had ever told her.

People remembered her brother. It made things a little easier. A bad reputation in their town went a long, long way.

Spider began to walk to school with Kayla, who had waist-length black hair and was one of the prettiest girls in seventh grade. She just sat there when the boys fawned over her and already looked weary of it all. Her group was Shana, who was a half-Japanese

dirtbags > 107

bully, and Diana, a chubby blonde who ran the student council like a small dictatorship, both rich girls from Crown Heights. Kayla was poorer than everyone, even Spider, and wore incredibly ugly clothes that had been passed down to her from her equally ragamuffin sisters. Gossip was used like currency. Spider realized that for some reason, people liked to tell her things.

Sometimes in the hallway Spider saw Amy Flowers. She'd developed acne and hardly had any friends. Spider gave her long, hard looks and Amy scurried past every time.

Things were happening in Spider's house. She and her mother went shopping for her first bra. "What do you need that for," Johnny teased. "To cover your mosquito bites?"

The boys at school snapped her bra elastic while she clamped down her teeth and endured. Johnny started working in a garage doing clean up and oil changes. He never seemed to be home and Spider's father was always at work. She and her mother circled each other cautiously.

It was a Saturday morning and Spider's stomach had cramped for hours. She went to the bathroom to pee and saw blood in her underwear. Her period was finally on her, another hassle, like having new boobs that were hard and always sore. She vowed to bleed to death before asking her mother for help. Spider read the instructions on the tampon box and eased one in. She walked out to the living room. Her mother ironed and watched TV, a talk show hosted by a grating redhead.

"I'm on the rag," Spider said.

"What?"

"I got my *period*." Her mother jumped and put down the iron, came toward her open-armed. When Spider saw the look on her face she thought *Yikes* and backed down the hallway.

"You're a woman now," she said.

"Gross," Spider said, and raced back to the bathroom, locking the door.

Her mother knocked softly. "Do you need anything? Rosie?"

"NO! Mom, just don't tell dad and Johnny. Please," she begged through the door. "I don't want them to know."

At dinnertime Spider's father wouldn't meet her eyes and Johnny kept smirking. "This roast beef is bloody," he said, pushing down his fork on the slab of meat. "Just look at all this blooood."

"Shut up," her mother said. Her father didn't say a word while they ate. Spider felt like something had changed in her family. It had passed without a ripple, but left an earthquake shaking inside her.

Her father never sat her on his lap again.

36

At lunch Spider sat with Kayla and her friends at the park across from the school. Their first formal dance of Grade 8 was that night. It was all they'd talked about for weeks.

"I hope Mr. Theissen is gonna be there," Kayla said. "I don't care if he's the gym teacher, he's so hot."

"Ho-leeee, old!"

"Ho-leee, *cute*!"

"Mark's coming over here," Diana said, straightening up. There was a flurry of activity. Mark played baseball and was one of the cutest boys in the school. He spun the bars of the merry-go-round and jumped on beside Spider. The girls all seemed to lean forward at once.

"Hey Spider," he said. "Greg wants to know if you wanna go to the dance with him tonight." Greg was the official class bully. Spider had made out with him a week before when they'd crashed Diana's birthday party. Johnny had bootlegged a bottle of vodka for Spider. Everyone at the party had got drunk in Diana's basement then opened the tiny bottles of liquor that decorated the back shelf of the empty bar. Shana threw up and Diana passed out in the kitty litter. Kayla had made out in the closet with Mark and he'd never talked to her again.

Spider wished she had never kissed Greg. His mouth had tasted sour. She shook her head no. "I can't," she said. "I'm going with my friends."

"It's like a date," Mark said impatiently. "He'll pick you up at your house." Kayla mouthed *say YES* and Diana kept nodding her head at her.

"No," Spider said and motioned to the girls. "We're all going together."

A few other boys came over. Mark jumped off and they started to spin the merry-go-round.

"They don't go out with boys 'cause they're gay!"

"Mark, WE'RE not," Kayla said quickly.

The boys spun the merry-go-round faster and faster. Diana whined and almost puked. Spider's hands were so sweaty she didn't know how much longer she could hang on.

"Lesbos!"

"It's the Rub Club!"

Finally they left and the merry-go-round stopped. Diana's face was green. "Thanks a lot Spider," Kayla said. "You just totally ruined my chances with Mark."

The girls walked fast all the way back to school. They didn't look at Spider. In class she stared at her books so hard she thought her eyes would break. After school no one had waited for her at the bike racks. She walked home alone. When she opened the door her mother said, "How did school go today?"

"It went fine," Spider answered.

During dinner Spider tried to think of a reason for not going to the formal, even though she had a ticket and her mother had bought her new dress pants and shoes. Johnny's best friend Tucker was over, eating his second piece of fried chicken. Spider took a deep breath. "I don't think the formal—"

Johnny interrupted to tell about the girl who had kicked Tucker in the balls at the last high school dance.

"Watch your mouth," their mother warned.

"I was just dancing with her," Tucker protested.

"If some girl kneed ME in the balls, I'd try to figure out what the hell I was doing wrong," Johnny laughed. At the end of the table Tucker shoveled mashed potatoes into his mouth and turned red.

"I don't want to go to the dance anymore." Spider said.

"I spent sixty dollars on that outfit," her mother said. "You're going." She told Spider to go to her room until it was time to leave and threatened to curl her hair.

Johnny was learning how to drive and he and their father gave Spider a ride. All the way there they talked about carburetors. When they got to the school parking lot she started to tell them she'd changed her mind but then her father turned around and said, "Spider, you look real nice."

In the dim light of the gym Spider saw her friends sitting on the paper-streamed bleachers. She waved and walked over. "Hi guys," she said. No one said anything. The silence was thick and horrible. Kayla looked at her feet. Shana whispered to Diana, and then they all walked away. Spider stared after them. The music was loud and she sat on the top of the bleachers alone. No one asked her to dance.

Spider took off the flower her mother had pinned to her jacket, ripped it apart with her fingernails on the long walk home.

On Monday morning Kayla's mother came to the front door and said, "Kayla does not want you to pick her up for school anymore, *Spider.*" Spider stared at Mrs. Sinclair's red feet, cruelly jammed in her plastic sandals. The door slammed shut in her face.

Diana and Kayla looked straight ahead when they passed Spider in the hallway. Shana hit her open locker door with her shoulder whenever she walked by. Spider ate her lunch in a bathroom stall and read the graffiti over and over. Anytime the door swung open she held her breath. The hours in school crept past.

She learned to have a book handy to read in the long, lonely minutes between classes and before school started. In the library she found out how to make a bomb with the celluloid scraped from the backs of playing cards.

Christmas vacation started. Her mother made pans of sugar cookies and shortbread. At night her father plugged the car into a block heater so it would start in the morning. There was so much snow the front walk had to be shoveled a few times a day.

Johnny broke his leg the first week on the hill, skiing back woods with his friends. It was a clean break that would be easy to heal. He mostly sat propped in the living room with his cast on a pillow in front of the television.

He and Spider watched a movie about a killer grizzly. It was Friday night and outside a bunch of guys walked down the street, amped up from drinking in the park and looking for a fight. "Get them before they get us!" one of them yelled, and they took off.

It was almost ten and their parents were already asleep. A commercial came on for adult diapers. Spider counted the days left of vacation before school started again, and then recounted to be sure. She watched Johnny across the room and wondered what he'd do in her situation. If someone didn't like him he might try to figure it out and then it would probably never bother him again.

"Corn chips smell like dog fur," Johnny said, cramming a handful in his mouth. "Ever notice that?" It had been a long time since something seemed funny and that made Spider start to cry. It was sudden and terrible. Johnny stopped mid-reach for the chip bowl. "What's wrong, Spider?" he asked, completely bewildered.

"I don't have any friends," she sobbed. "Anymore."

"Whaddya talking about?" he said. She could not explain the intricacies and delicate power balances between teenage girls. Johnny wouldn't comprehend it. He'd been friends with Tucker since elementary school. He was on the ski team and played basketball and everyone liked him.

"Shana and Diana got mad because I wouldn't go to the dance with this boy. And now they don't want to be friends with me anymore."

"What guy?"

"It doesn't matter."

"Shana? What about Kayla?"

Spider told him how Mrs. Sinclair had slammed the door in her face. Johnny looked at Spider as she cried and shoved soggy chips in her mouth. A car horn beeped outside.

"That's Tucker," he said. "We're going to the hockey game. Are you gonna be okay?"

dirtbags > 113

Spider shrugged and wiped her eyes.

"Put your boots on," he said. "You're coming with us."

Hockey games were a big event. Everyone walked around the stands or watched the game in the seats and drank out of flasks in their pockets. There were always parties afterward. Spider stood at the top of the bleachers with Johnny and a group of his friends. Everyone stopped by to sign his cast. Shana and Kayla walked by, staring.

"Hey you little bitches," Johnny said. "Where do you think you're going?"

Tucker cornered them against the wall and Johnny swung over on his crutches. Spider couldn't hear what was going on but she could tell he was angry. Finally Tucker let them pass.

"What'd you say to them?" Spider asked Johnny when he came back.

"I told them to leave you alone and then Tucker jumped in and said if they didn't he'd beat them up."

"Little preppie bitches," Tucker said.

"No one treats my little sister like that," Johnny said. After the game they went home and he fell asleep on the couch. The grizzly movie was over and now there was one on about aliens. After that Spider watched part of a scary stalker movie her mother would never have let her see. She had a feeling that her problems in school were over.

37

Spider spent the summer before high school working in a video store. Sometimes she played Dungeons and Dragons with the owner's son, Jeff, until the day he had her character, a warrior queen, raped by a band of elves. The owner's name was Linda and she spent her time in the coffee shop down the street, so Spider was mostly alone. No one ever came in. Linda paid Spider five dollars an hour and she got to watch all the movies she wanted.

The first day at Woodlands Secondary Spider darted down the hallway with the other Grade 9 kids. For one brief moment everyone in her grade was united because they could tell already that high school was scary and going to be full of hard knocks. Spider's classmates were generally a dull lot, and they followed each other in a timid herd.

"That's Johnny's little sister," a girl sang in the hallway. "Hi Spider!" It was a senior named Tashi who had gone out with Johnny for a while in tenth grade. Girls had always called for Johnny. They liked his sly smile and kind eyes. Tashi had braided Spider's hair when they'd sat and watched TV. She'd been one of Spider's favourites.

"Hey, look at the little Mackenzie," some guy said to his friends. "It's a girl!"

Johnny was a popular senior and everybody knew him, even the janitors. If a car squealed coming into the parking lot or laid rubber when it left, chances were he'd be in it. He spent his time in shop class, where the tools fit easily into his hands. When he got his license he'd driven doughnuts around a crowd of kids waiting for the bus. No one had been hurt so he'd only

dirtbags > 115

been suspended from school for three days. Another time he was suspended for stapling a boy's arm in Typing class.

Everybody loved Johnny. Jocks and rockers respected him equally. He was good at sports, but on weekends he partied with metal heads. He was an all-around nice guy, his life seemed comfortable and smooth like he had decided early on that nothing would bother him much, and because of this had kind words for everyone.

At home Johnny and Spider never talked about school. It seemed best to let their parents know as little as possible about their lives. During dinner they ate their plates of meat and potatoes and vegetables. This never varied and there were rules. Drink a full glass of milk and eat everything you took. Their mother picked the bones clean and watched them with keen eyes. It was the one time during the day when she had the family together. They swallowed quickly. Their father usually watched the TV while he ate. Sometimes he warned them to change their attitudes. After dinner he read the paper then fell asleep in his chair.

When Johnny wasn't home Spider sat in her room alone.

One day at school a girl cornered Spider in the bathroom. "You're Johnny's sister, right?" Her name was Yvonne. She wore skin-tight jeans and had a big horse face. She'd tripped Spider once in the hallway.

Spider nodded and finished washing her hands. "So, does he have a girlfriend?" Yvonne smelled like cigarette smoke and Love's Baby Soft. A piece of pink gum swelled in the corner of her mouth.

Spider watched her in the mirror. "If I were you I'd forget it," she said. "You don't have a chance with my brother." Yvonne's mouth stayed open mid-chew.

"You're a weirdo bitch," she said, but not very loud.

Spider walked toward the door. "Don't ever fucken talk to me again," she said. She wasn't afraid of any girl in her school.

38

Most mornings Spider stalled at her locker before classes and that usually made her late. As she hurried down the hall one morning Greg passed by with one of his friends. He knocked the books out of Spider's arms and kicked her binder. It broke against a locker. "QUIT IT," she said. "You asshole!" "Asshole," they mimicked. Their laughter echoed all the way down the hallway.

Spider went to the bathroom on the second floor near the science labs and stared in a mirror, trying to figure out what was wrong with her. She had two eyes, a nose, and a mouth. She looked like a normal girl. There were no problems with her body. Her dark hair was straight and long, she had some freckles she kind of liked. She wondered if she needed to wear make-up. Spider noticed a pimple on her chin and suddenly felt ugly. Monstrous. The thought of trying to make it through the next three and a half years made her face crumple. At the sink she pressed a ball of wet paper towel against her red cheeks.

The door swung open. Spider straightened up and wiped her eyes. It embarrassed her to be caught crying. The girl went into a stall. It was Jenny White, who Spider once heard had worn a bra since third grade. When she came back out Jenny asked, "Are you okay?" Spider had gone to school with her for years and they'd never spoken.

"Fuck," Spider said, throwing away the paper towel. "No."

Jenny looked at her a moment. "You want to go have a cigarette?"

Spider had never smoked at school before. There were very clear demarcation lines between who went to the smoke area and who didn't. Plus, she'd always been scared because she didn't know what Johnny would say if he saw her there. But she didn't care that day.

"Let's go," Spider said.

The smoking area was a banged up picnic table just past the parking lot behind the school. A couple of burnout kids stood around. Jenny gave her a cigarette.

"Do you like high school?" Spider asked her.

"The teachers suck. Let's see—there's Mr. Ritter, an old alcoholic who sleeps in class."

"I've got Mr. Marsh for English," Spider said. "He looks down the girl's shirts."

"And they probably like it."

Jenny was a short, big-nosed blonde with a sparkle in her blue eyes. Spider tried not to look at her chest. Jenny had the biggest boobs she'd ever seen.

"It's the school of six hundred hicks," Spider said, even though she didn't know how many people went to the school and had no real basis for any comparison.

"We'd better go," Jenny said. "I was right about you. Any girl named Spider has to be cool." Spider felt ashamed that Jenny was so nice and she'd always ignored her. When Spider got to class the teacher yelled at her for being so late then yelled again because she was smiling.

Spider was putting her books away after school when Jenny stopped by her locker. "Hey, do you want to go for coffee?"

"Sure," Spider said. "Mister Burger?"

"Yeah," Jenny said. "But let's make a quick stop first."

They stood behind the trees at the edge of the parking lot and smoked a joint. Jenny White had really good weed that she stole from her mom. She said if her mom smoked too much of it she had to go hide in the closet because it made her so paranoid. Spider told her she and Johnny were trying to grow marijuana plants in egg cartons in his room. They walked past the rugby team practicing on the field.

"Look at that guy!"

"Who?"

"Holy shit, he's gone commando. Hey 23!" Jenny yelled. "We can see your CHUNK!" The boy looked up red-faced and checked his shorts. That cracked them up. Then Jenny said, "So, why were you crying this morning?"

"Oh," Spider said, embarrassed again. "Just feeling bad about myself."

"You? You're so pretty and nice," Jenny said, bewildered. "What do you have to feel bad about?" It made Spider smile. Jenny really was a sweetheart.

They debated their favourite heavy metal singers and talked of being in a band. At Mister Burger they drank coffee, chain-smoked, and played game after game of tabletop Ms. Pacman at the back of the restaurant. Jenny wanted to get so good she could eventually break the machine.

"Hey, you going to the game tonight? I can get some booze from my mom," Jenny said, yanking the joystick. "Wanna come with?"

"Yeah," Spider said. "Hell yeah."

They met at the entrance to the arena. Jenny's cousin Charlene was out drinking in the parking lot. Jenny and Spider sat in the bleachers for a while then stood in line for more hot chocolate to mix with their rum. It was a large crowd at the concession stand and Shana and Kayla butted ahead of them.

"*Excuse* me," Jenny said, and pushed back in front of them. "Don't be so fucking rude."

"Oh my god," Kayla said to Spider. "Are you hanging out with *her?*" She jabbed her finger toward Jenny.

Spider said, "Fuck off!"

"What's *your* problem?" Kayla's frosted lips pulled back. Spider wondered how she'd ever thought she was pretty.

"You're MY problem," Jenny said in a loud voice. "The problem is that you need to close your legs. Because Kayla, you are one stinky cheese." Shana and Kayla moved back into the crowd. "We all smell you, Kayla!" They ducked their heads and pushed faster.

Spider and Jenny got the hot chocolates and walked back to the bleachers. "Shana Tamasuki...rhymes with dookie," Spider said.

"A fecal-philliac!"

"She's into scat."

"I've *never* liked jazz," Jenny said.

When they stopped laughing Jenny put her arm across Spider's shoulders. "If anyone ever gives you trouble, you come and tell *me*," she said.

Spider learned about the loyalty of girls. Again.

39

Jenny was like no fifteen-year-old girl Spider had ever seen. When she walked down the hallway people paid attention because they couldn't stop staring at her breasts. "My boobs come into the room before I do," she liked to say. She was smarter than anyone gave her credit for. Spider's mother had disliked her immediately. Jenny went with Spider for smoke breaks, even though she'd quit. Spider's own cigarette habit was developing nicely.

They liked to party at Jenny's house because they drank with her mom and stole her pot. Her dad had left when she was a baby and Jenny lived downstairs with her mother's eight cats. The house was covered in kittens and fur and smelled of cat piss. Every day after school Jenny played with the cats. She liked to dance with them and the cats seemed to like it, too. She knew their names and every single habit and wanted to graduate so she could be a veterinarian assistant. Jenny was so poor the walls weren't insulated, and in the winter the icicles grew almost as big as her house. The hallways were an obstacle course of yowling cats and space heaters.

In their small town everyone knew Jenny and her mom: chubby, cheerful blondes who liked to party. Spider had heard what people had said about Jenny White—that she was a dim-witted, over-developed girl. Jenny suspected her mother used to be a stripper, and there were men coming in and out of their house behind the gas station all day. Sometimes Jenny met strangers at work or went home with grown men to get high in their dirty kitchens. She'd lost her virginity in the sixth grade.

Jenny gave Spider an old leather jacket and it was the coolest thing she owned. They wore sneakers and tight jeans and shirts with ugly bands on the front. Spider put streaks in her hair and re-read the same metal magazines. Already she felt disappointed by the world. Her music got louder. She talked to Jenny for hours on the phone after she'd seen her all day. They poured any liquor they could find down their throats. Spider lay in bed and dreamed about boys. Her earphones were always on. She screamed into her pillow. She ruined things that other people put care and time into. She was bored. She didn't know why she hated her mother.

She was a teenage girl.

Jenny and Spider bought a gram of hash from Dustin Drake outside the library then went up to the top floor fire exit where it was easy to get to the roof. It was a Friday night and ninth grade was finally over. Johnny managed to get enough credits to graduate and already had full-time work at the garage. Jenny burned the bottom of the hash ball and crumbled it into the joint. They took deep drags of smoke and looked out at the town. "I wish we were graduating too," Spider said.

"And getting the fuck out of this town," Jenny agreed. The hash slowed everything down. Colours stood out in the darkness. The good taste of cigarette smoke and barbecue chips in Spider's mouth overwhelmed her, just like the cars that pulled off the highway into the bright lights of the 7-Eleven.

"You and I will be famous one day," she said. "We'll move to New York City and get matching tattoos." The words had just come out of her mouth when a meteor burned across the sky with a tail of red and orange fire, impossible to miss.

During the summer Spider stashed her bike at Jenny's and they hitchhiked to the lake when Jenny didn't have to work at the gas station. There were a lot of boys vacationing in cabins with their families. Usually they never stayed more than a week and Spider met her first boyfriend there, a dry-mouthed teenager named Rudy. They spent a lot of time kissing in hidden places where his mother always seemed to find them. When he went back to Port Moody he called Spider's house for a few weeks and made her talk to his friends to prove she was real.

School started again. Spider missed seeing Johnny there but he was still living in the basement. All through fall and winter he worked long hours in the shop.

The garage was filled with car parts, tires, and tools. Johnny was rebuilding the engine in the car he was restoring, a '65 Chevy Nova. His license had been suspended for two years for stealing a jeep and ramming through the front of the town bowling alley. Because of this everyone called him "Pins." Since Johnny was one of the best mechanics in town the cops never stopped him from driving.

Some nights Johnny helped Jenny and Spider with their homework. He could take stuff that had seemed hard in class and explain it in a way that didn't make them feel dumb. Then they'd all cram on the couch and watch the Discovery channel stoned. Sometimes he bought them liquor and Jenny traded him for weed.

When Spider turned sixteen in April her parents gave her fifty dollars and, inexplicably, a garment bag. Jenny bought two hits of acid from her cousin Charlene. Spider was nervous—they'd heard the story of the kid who'd freaked out so bad his friends had left him in a shopping cart on his parent's front yard and run away. It was dusk and they chewed the tiny squares of paper in Jenny's bedroom. After a while everything seemed tilted and then the whole room began to twinkle and shiver with lights. Spider communicated intensely with the kitten Mr. Fibs, and Jenny, and then individual houseplants. They were hysterical with laughter because tiny polka dots danced above the pillowcase on the bed.

Johnny's present was driving lessons. He had finished rebuilding his muscle car. It was painted metallic blue with white trim. He proudly showed her the Hurst gearshift and 283 engine and Cragar wheels. Their mother hated the spare parts, grease and dirty fingernails. Everything was a conspiracy to ruin her backyard and yellow the grass.

When Spider got her license Johnny sometimes let her take out his car. She drove down the highway fast, music loud, and for the first time she really believed that one day she'd get out of that town. Whenever she revved the engine and pulled out of the driveway it always made her smile.

40

The party was in a house where three hockey players lived who had graduated years before. Johnny said things usually turned pretty wild. He was leaving for trade school in a few days and Spider had to keep asking but finally he said she and Jenny could come with him to the party.

The house was crowded and the living room stereo played old rock music: Jimi Hendrix and The Doors and Cream. One of the hockey players, Jamie, was blonde and very cute. He stood close to Spider in the kitchen. "I can't believe your name is Spider," he kept asking. "Is it really?" When her glass was empty Jamie grabbed her hand and led her to the keg. He pumped Spider another plastic cup of beer like a real gentleman.

Spider didn't realize Jamie was actually flirting until he put his arm across her shoulders. Another beer, another trip to the keg. Spider felt his hand touching her ass. She began to get drunk and he started to look even cuter.

"C'mon," he said into her ear. "Let's go up to my room." She followed him through the party. Outside on the back porch a couple groped each other. The girl had her shirt open. It was Jenny White. The boy she was with was a stranger.

Jamie took Spider's hand and led her upstairs. He closed the door to his room. Spider felt like she had to lose her virginity sooner or later. It seemed like a good enough time. She gulped the rest of her beer and they started making out on the bed.

His mouth slid wetly over her face and neck and everything moved too fast. Jamie pulled down Spider's clothes and all she could feel was her naked skin in the cold room. The weight of him on her chest was too heavy. His cock stabbed frantically between her legs.

"No," Spider said, and tried to get up. "I don't...want to anymore." Jamie jerked up her legs and pinned back her arms. He pushed into her and it hurt. Spider took it and thought she would vomit.

When her hands were free she covered her face and couldn't stop crying. "C'mon," Jamie grunted. "Make an effort." He pounded into her even harder.

Finally it was over. Spider got up and scrambled around in the dark for her clothes, horrified she couldn't find her panties. They were hot pink and matched her bra. She imagined Jamie showing them to his friends the next day. In the bathroom mirror her face was a horror show, red eyes and giant black streaks of makeup. She scrubbed her skin hard with a towel.

Spider came out and walked stiffly down the hallway. The door to Jamie's bedroom was open and he still lay in bed. "Hey," he called as she went past. "Thanks for a great birthday present."

Someone changed the record in the living room. Spider reeled through the party and found Jenny. As soon as she saw Spider's face she put her hand on her shoulder and walked her out to the car.

Jenny asked, "Do you want to leave?" Spider crawled into the back seat and whimpered. "Stay here," she said. "I'm getting Johnny." After awhile Johnny opened the car door and asked her if she was okay.

Spider lay on the backseat, shivering. "Please just take me home."

Johnny started the car and drove down the rain-slicked street. He kept twisting around to look at her. "What's the matter with you?" He turned to Jenny. "What the hell happened?"

"I don't know," Jenny said. "I don't."

Johnny pulled the car over and climbed into the back seat. "Spider, I'm not going anywhere until I find out what's wrong." The look on his face was absolute. Something inside her broke loose.

"I went upstairs with Jamie," she sobbed. "And I let him take off my clothes. But then I wanted him to stop and he wouldn't."

The shame was so huge she stared at the carpet. She stared at the floor mat and her shoes, anywhere but Johnny's eyes. Everything in the world depended on how he looked at her. Johnny climbed into the front seat and turned the car around. He didn't say a word. He drove back to the party and parked out front. "Stay here," he told them. He got the tire iron out of the trunk and went into the house. A few minutes later he came back out and got into the car. He didn't have the iron anymore.

That morning Jamie left town. Spider bled into her underwear for three days.

41

Summer ended and Johnny left for trade school. Spider and Jenny went to parties and stood around bonfires, listening to heavy metal blast out of truck stereos into the woods. They drank in playgrounds and in parking lots, climbed Black Mountain and partied at the water tower. Sometimes Spider was allowed to take her parent's car. She loved to pick up Jenny in the mornings on the days she decided to go to school. Jenny would jump in the car with her hair wet as Spider turned the stereo up louder. During lunch hour they cruised the town. One night they drank in the park and smoked hash oil with the car lighter, then sped down the highway, so high they thought they saw the Reaper in the shadows just above the headlights. The white lines blurred, everything shone dark blue in the moonlight. Jenny gripped the dashboard, laughed and screamed at the same time. "I'm fucked up," she said.

"We're sixteen," Spider said. "This is what we do."

When Johnny finished his course he moved to a bigger town a few hours west. He got a job fixing machinery at the ski hill. It was hard not having her brother around. Jenny started dating her neighbour, a large-headed man named Ken whom Spider despised. Jenny had only been at school half the time, and now she came even less. Their school had a policy that if you missed three classes without a note (or a fairly plausible excuse) then you got a three-day suspension, which resulted in even more free time. There were so many kids crowded into the school that the system was gloriously lax.

There was nothing else for Spider to do but study. The grades she got were decent and it surprised her to find that some of what they said in class could actually be sifted through and found useful. The idea of going to college or university did not seem so absurd. Spider worked hard. Her only plan was to get out of town, just like her brother. It didn't matter how.

Finally, it was senior year. For the first time everyone in their class put aside their judgments and petty snobbery and got together—to celebrate the fact that they were done with high school and would never have to see each other again.

Spider applied to every college and university that would take her. Mr. Newton, the school counselor, helped her fill out scholarship forms after school. He was a hairy-armed, bald-headed man who wore thick glasses. He liked to talk about his son, Billy the Fuck-up, who Spider had known since junior high. Their lockers were assigned alphabetically and always near each other. Spider got a full one-year scholarship to a school seven hundred miles away. All the hours spent writing until her hand cramped, photocopying forms, and pretending to listen to Mr. Newton had really paid off.

Billy Newton stood at Spider's locker after school, shuffling his feet nervously. "Hi Spider," he said. Billy was a tall, skinny rocker with long hair and always wore death metal shirts. He was seen as one of the troubled kids in school. Sometimes he sold joints for five dollars in the smoking area. Whenever he and Spider talked they made fun of his dad.

"Hi Billy."

"Hey uh, you wanna go to the prom with me?" Billy stared at her collarbone and blushed. Spider remembered he had once burped in her face in sixth grade.

Spider had thought about going. "It'll probably suck," she said. Billy's face dropped and she recovered. "But I think you'd make it fun."

Billy smiled then, and looked like a different person. Spider was pleased someone had asked her. Jenny was taking her boyfriend Ken, the twenty-four-year-old construction worker, and in Spider's opinion he had a personality disorder that manifested itself in his grossly over-sized head. Billy said he would buy the tickets and they figured out what time for him to pick her up. Shana and Kayla walked by, smirking.

"Oh my god," Shana said. "It's the Burnout Queen and Billy the Skid." Kayla cackled loudly. Billy mumbled something, red-faced, and took off down the hall. Spider shut her locker door and sighed. That was the world. They took something gentle and made it as ugly as they could.

Billy brought Spider a corsage the length of her arm and had a case of beer in the front seat of the car. Spider's mother had given her a bit of money for a dress and all she could find was a horrible blue number with oily layers of satin she'd altered at home. Worst of all was that she had a matching jacket she'd worn to her own prom and so desperately wanted Spider to wear it she couldn't refuse. Spider ditched it right away. On the way to the prom Billy blasted Judas Priest so loud the windows rattled. His eyes were bloodshot. Halfway through the night he left the dance to go to 7-Eleven with his friends and never came back. Jenny and Spider drank rye out of her flask while she sat on Ken's lap and he ogled the teenage girls.

"Billy and I didn't even dance," Spider said. "I didn't expect much but…I mean, he left with my jacket in the back of his car."

"Best night of our lives," Jenny said. "What crap."

Spider walked over to Billy's a few days later to get the jacket. She didn't want to see him or Mr. Newton, but her mother had become hysterical she'd lost it. A young man opened the door. It was Dave Newton, Billy's older brother. He had graduated in the same class as Johnny and Spider remembered that in high school he drank so much booze his nickname was "Juice." Dave was skinny too, and had weird curls that sprung out from his head. He looked like a mama's boy from the wrong side of mama.

"Billy's not here," he said. He was eating a banana and threw the peel in the bushes. "I just stopped by but no one was home." Dave said he had a place across town and they chatted for a while on the porch. "What's Johnny doing these days?" he asked.

"Working over in Riverside," Spider said.

"What about you?"

"I'm going to school in September."

Dave had attended the same school, a liberal university with a large arts program. He had gone for a semester and been kicked out because he'd drank too much beer and never went to class.

"I really need a summer job," Spider said. "My scholarship barely covers tuition."

"There's an opening where I work," Dave said. "A waitress quit yesterday. Go down right now to Caesar's Steakhouse and ask for Phil. C'mon, I'll give you a ride."

"Thanks," Spider said. They headed to his truck. Spider was beginning to notice Dave was a cute boy. On the way to the restaurant he asked if she was dating his brother. "Hell no," she said.

"Good," Dave said. He was serious. "My brother is bad news."

The owner of the restaurant was a tall epileptic named Phil. "Do you have any experience?" he asked. Spider lied easily. Helping her mother wait on her father and brother seemed like work experience enough. Phil gave Spider a red apron and a pad and told her she had a split shift the next day.

It was an easy job, slow and steady in the restaurant except at the end of the night after the movie ended. The theatre was across the street. For two hours they would be slammed, orders flying out, and when they closed the staff got drunk in the demolished kitchen. After work Dave would ask Spider if she needed a ride somewhere. It always went the same. "I live really close, Dave."

"You want a ride anyway?"

One night she told Dave he could drive her to Jenny's. Spider's feet and back ached but it had been a good shift and she had a roll of bills in tips. She invited Dave to Jenny's, too. He took a bottle of vodka and a case of beer from the kitchen cooler. Spider started to forget about her sore feet and wondered how her hair looked.

Jenny was already drunk in the kitchen when they got there. She cracked a can of beer and raised it high. Her mother was out of town with her new boyfriend and the house was unusually messy. "Hey," Spider said. "What are you doing?"

"What am I doing?" Jenny asked, spreading her arms wide. "What am I doing? THIS." She took a large gulp of beer. "Here's to…ME!"

Ken had dumped her the day after the prom. Jenny said she wasn't upset about it, but Spider wasn't sure. They all sat at the table listening to music and drank a mixture of vodka, orange juice, 7-Up and lemon. Spider put a layer of maraschino cherries in the bottom of her glass. "That's fruit cocktail," Dave said. "It's like jam with booze in it."

They played dice and quarters. Dave turned the stereo louder and they danced with the cats. Jenny got so drunk she puked on her mom's curtains. Dave cleaned everything up while Spider talked her out of calling Ken before she passed out. Spider and Dave smoked a joint and then curled up on the couch together.

A few nights later Jenny went out partying with a group of boys up at a cabin on the other side of Black Mountain. The cabin was on the back property of a weird farm kid who sometimes rode his horse into town. The boys gave her shot after shot of tequila and made sure she passed out. They took off Jenny's clothes and arranged her in poses with each other. There was a camera. They did bad things to her. Jenny woke up when they started to shave her.

When the stories got out Jenny left town. She didn't tell anyone, just got on a bus and left. It destroyed her mother completely.

42

Spider spent a lot of time with Dave. There was the swimming hole and barbecues and blankets at the drive-in. It was so hot that July the gravel roads turned white. All summer there was talk of war. Billy Newton had left town after he'd found out she was dating his brother.

One night Spider sat at the staff table and smoked, waiting for Dave to finish his shift. When they worked together he made Spider dishes of baked cheese on her break and left her joints with little notes. Phil's brother was there to eat for free as usual, and kept looking back and forth between them. Finally he went into the kitchen. "What's this?" he yelled at Dave. "That your girlfriend?"

"Yep," Dave said from the kitchen.

"She looks fourteen years old!"

"Yeah," she heard Dave say. "Ain't it great?"

Spider liked that boy.

Dave lived in an apartment with his friend Derek, who was even older and worked as a logger. It was Derek's place and his girlfriend Valerie pretty much lived there, too. She had curly black hair and a double chin. When Valerie found out Spider had just graduated from high school she looked at Spider like she was a bug that had dropped onto her shoe.

Most nights after work Spider and Dave went to the lake and sat in his truck, just talking. Once they started kissing they didn't want to stop. Spider always told her parents she'd worked late cleaning up. They wouldn't have minded, she had just turned

dirtbags > 133

eighteen after all, but she didn't want to deal with her mother's questions and expectations.

Dave and Spider went to the movies one night. Spider actually wore a dress. All through the film he joked and tried to put his hand up her skirt. She tried to act demure. "You even shined your toes up!" he said when he saw her red-painted toenails. She knew something was going to happen that night.

Back at the apartment they lay on his bed, talked and stroked each other. Spider told him about Jamie, the party, the screeching guitar and the blood. Dave promised to be gentle. They undressed each other and took their time. Spider knew she was ready.

Dave said it would feel good and it did, like an ache had finally stopped hurting. But Spider stayed awake long after he had fallen asleep. Without that pain there was a strange, foreign space inside her.

It was the end of August and Spider would soon leave for school. Dave was getting serious. Spider knew he wanted her to stay. Sometimes she imagined her life with him: their apartment and community college, a dog and then a house and his truck and their kids. Spider saw him with thinning hair and a fat belly, how she would love him still. Yet Spider knew what she truly wanted was the one thing Dave couldn't give her. Experience.

One night they sat in Dave's living room listening to music. Derek and his girlfriend had gone camping for the weekend. Spider stretched out across the couch to light a joint. She was naked except for Dave's Triumph T-shirt, her dark hair half in a braid.

"You're so beautiful," he said. Spider laughed. "I can't let you go," he said. "Please don't leave me."

Spider stopped laughing. Beneath the music, the silence was huge.

Dave carried her bags to the truck. Spider's parents had given her a set of luggage for a graduation present and five hundred dollars. Everything left in her room she'd already packed in boxes.

It was too early in the morning to say goodbye. Her father was already at work, and had given her an extra fifty dollars for pocket money the night before. Her mother began to fry bacon and eggs but Spider was hung-over and the smell of grease made her stomach roll. Spider said her and Dave would eat on the road and her mother's face got tight.

"Fine!" she said, and slammed down the spatula. "Drive on an empty stomach and get into an accident!" Spider went out to the truck and her mother waited in her bathrobe on the porch until Dave started the engine. Spider waited to feel bad about leaving, but didn't. Maybe it was all the times her mother had yelled, "I can't *wait* till you're out of my house!"

The university was forty-five minutes away from a medium-sized city. Dave pointed out different buildings on campus. Spider found it quite amazing that he had been kicked out of school for failing every single one of his classes. Dave laughed hard when he re-lived the old kegger days. Student Orientation consisted of a guided tour of the campus, free lunch, and early sign-up for freshmen. Dave said it would be worth it, just to avoid any eight a.m. classes. He had already warned her to bring as much food from home as she could.

They watched the sky change colours through the windshield of his truck until it finally stayed black. Spider fell asleep in the front seat with Dave's arm curled around her. It had been a good day.

Dave and Spider said goodbye that night in the silence of his truck. The next morning he dropped her off at school. He had been her first love and it was hard to let that go. They never saw each other again.

She remembered he drove away slow.

43

Spider had been assigned to the worst dorm in student housing.

There were four identical buildings in each quad, three floors in each building. The four dormitories were social, academic, varsity, and first year. Each room had a window, bed, desk, and closet. Because Spider was a scholarship student she didn't have a choice of where she stayed. Her floor housed most of the school basketball team, the Warlords. They were also known as the Whorelords because of the groupies that trailed after them. A favourite joke of the Warlords was to take a shit in someone's room, then turn up the heat and lock the door. The girls on the floor were all basketball fans, and it made Spider very suspicious.

She was almost finished unpacking her room when someone yelled "FLOOR MEETING! EVERYONE IN THE LOUNGE!" The resident advisor, a toothy biology student named Steve, gave out maps of the fire exits and warned them not to light candles in the rooms. He then told them the story of a girl who'd been so high on mushrooms that she'd pulled the fire alarm and then hid in a closet. An older hippie student asked if there was recycling in the quad and somebody groaned. "I don't know about that," Steve smiled with his big, shiny teeth. "But I can tell you which bars have the best wet T-shirt night."

"HAW HAW," the boys roared. Spider noticed they were all dressed in sporting gear. Steve then had them go around the room in a circle and introduce themselves. Spider was too far from the door to slip out.

"My name is Shelley. I play volleyball and I want to be a physiotherapist."

"I'm Brad. I'm from Edmonton. I like to partay naked. Haw-haw! Yeah!"

Spider hands were sweaty and she went over in her head what she was going to say. Finally it was her turn. "My name is Spider. It really is. I come from a little town where cows tip over the people." There was a pause and someone belched. Everyone laughed. It was going to be a tough year.

The first semester Spider had Art History in a huge lecture hall with two hundred students. During class someone always farted or fell asleep snoring. It was the same place she had her Psychology and Anthropology classes. In Introduction to Literature the professor held up each of the ten novels the class was assigned to read that year. He had written one of them. The best class was a poetry workshop. The professor was a small blonde woman, and the first thing she said in class was that she had three beautiful sons and the youngest had just run away and joined the circus.

For the first time Spider truly enjoyed school—long afternoons in the library basement with a textbook and highlighter, copious lecture notes and research papers. A whole day could slip by her in a novel and she read every book the teachers assigned. Spider liked observing the people in her classes; suburban lesbians, bad-breathed bulimics, anarchists, even an odd genius or two. Everything she learned made the world open up a little more.

44

Christmas came and Spider took the bus home with the history of the Russian revolution and half the world in art. Johnny was going to stay a week over Christmas and she couldn't wait to see him.

Her brother was away on a ski trip with Tucker when Spider got home. She slept for a day and woke up happy. The fridge was full. She told her mother she was now a vegetarian. Her mother became furious and told Spider she was going to ruin Christmas dinner.

Spider had called Dave once before she got home. He was working avalanche patrol in the mountains and they wouldn't see each other. Spider wondered if he'd planned it that way.

"I'm always here for you Spider," he'd said. "I still love you." Spider knew it was true but didn't want him, and there was nothing she could do.

Spider waited for Johnny at the kitchen table with the light off. There was a bowl of fruit on the table. The plums were purple and rotting. Finally she heard his truck pull in. His blue ski jacket was still wet when he gave her a hug.

Johnny made a sandwich while they talked. He liked his job fixing machinery at the ski hill and rebuilding cars on the side, but had met a guy who worked on an oil patch in Calgary and said he could get Johnny on crew. The work was dangerous but a person could make a lot of money. Spider told Johnny about school and Dave. "Juice Newton?" he said, and laughed. She asked him how the Chevy was running, and the ski trip, if the old break still hurt his leg. They talked about living in a warm place, maybe Mexico or Florida. Somewhere sunny, they agreed. Spider had never liked winter and wouldn't miss the snow, at all.

45

Back at school Spider studied hard. No one around her ever seemed to go to class, except for aerobics. Soap operas were a major event. The girls hung out in the lounge and compared their fake suntans, did their nails, and watched TV while gossiping and disposing poorly thought-out advice to each other:

"Don't accept a date unless it's four days in advance. No, five!"

"If he tried to kiss *me* I'd press charges!"

The girls were pretty and brittle. They shopped with their student visas and put on make-up to go for dinner in the cafeteria. In the bathroom they shared obsessions over their weight and size of their asses, as well as the asses of various celebrities. The boys on the floor scrutinized the girls, planned maneuvers for them to be paraded and displayed. Basketball games were a huge event. Jock mentality ran the building. Date rape was a campus norm.

Spider's room was her sanctuary. She put up a picture of Dave at the lake; Jenny and her dressed like ninjas for Hallowe'en; the first photo she'd ever taken, of the cat Mrs. Kibbles; and a black and white portrait of Johnny looking young and impossibly handsome as he leaned against a splintered porch railing, smiling. "Who's that?" the girls cooed. Spider didn't like it when they tried to come into her room.

She spent a lot of time studying off-campus or smoking weed with the graduate hippie in his room. He had good information about police procedures and pot growing, but all he listened to was the Grateful Dead. It offended him when Spider told him the songs all sounded the same. He asked her to please leave his room.

A week before mid-terms Spider sat in the cafeteria eating lunch alone while coming off an all-nighter of caffeine and herbal speed. One of the nicer guys from her floor came over and sat down. His name was Sarge. He said he had a sister back home that he missed and a dog named Mick. He looked at the book she was reading for English class.

"What's this? 'A Doll's House'?"

"It's a horror story about a killer doll."

"Ibsen?" Sarge asked. "Never even heard of him. He must not be very good."

Sarge had tiny teeth and big lips and always wore jogging pants with no underwear. The girls nicknamed him Hung. He wanted to be a gym teacher, which Spider found hilarious. When she was dragged to dorm meetings or floor events, Sarge always maneuvered in next to her.

One night he came to her room, slightly drunk. "I had a bad day in class," he said. "The teacher read my answer out loud and said, 'You must've worked REALLY hard on this question! This is the stupidest thing I've ever heard!'"

Sarge was so upset over this humiliation that when he leaned into her Spider didn't have the heart to say no. They kissed for a while and then he pulled down his jogging pants. She touched his semi-soft cock. The condom was already on. There was a pause and Spider looked up at him. Then she laughed. Sarge got up, slamming the door when he left.

He sat with his friends in the cafeteria the next day. When Spider walked by he whispered something and they all started laughing. She sat down with her tray at a back table. Her hands trembled beside the cutlery and a pile of creamers. She wondered what he'd said that had been so funny. Finally they stopped laughing.

The girls in the dorm found out that the boys had a ratings board of them in their bathroom. They stormed it to make sure. Various boxes allowed the boys to judge the girl's tits, ass, dick-sucking abilities, and one for overall rank. All the boys wanted to fuck Ellie, a deeply tanned, vacant blonde. There was nothing in Spider's row except for two comments in the last box, where someone had written "Swamp Thing." Someone else had written, "Sloppy but nice." She found that quite touching.

In the lounge the girls clustered in noisy little groups. One girl, Giselle, was the loudest of all. She was a Business major and had an alarming mass of curls that dragged behind her.

"So I told Bob, 'That is soooo wrong to rate girls like that, with a scoreboard in the bathroom!' And he's like, 'Yeah, but you did good!'" A few minutes later she repeated the story to more girls who came into the lounge. Spider gave up trying to watch the news.

Susie started crying—she'd gotten a bunch of zeros on the board. The boys called her Grimace because she was a bit chubby and sometimes wore a purple tracksuit to breakfast. The girls crowded around her, patting her arms and shoulders. "Nooo, Susie, you are sooo pritty!" "Yah!" "I *love* your hair!" Susie wailed even louder.

On the Friday after mid-terms the building planned a floor crawl to celebrate. Spider's room was designated for beer funnels. She was alone, waiting for the next round when Sarge came in, drunk and slurring. In a sudden motion, as she turned to flick her cigarette butt out the window, he pulled her onto the bed, pushed her legs open with his knees. She was about to holler when the next group of partiers was laughing and beating on the door. Sarge fumbled with his pants and then Spider was up and out, running down the hall to the lounge. None of the girls would listen to her. Sarge was a popular guy.

The next day Sarge came to the door of her room and tried to apologize, grey-faced and sober. She said, "Stay the *fuck* away from me." She told him she had a brother. She told him he'd be sorry if he didn't.

46

Simone Ladeucer came right up to Spider one day after poetry workshop. "I liked your poem," she said. "And in this class I never like anything." The professor had asked them to write about their earliest memory. Some people read poems about potty training, or playing in the grass, or strawberry jam on a silver spoon. Spider wrote about breaking a toy in her room. It was a red paddle with a rubber ball attached by a long elastic string. Johnny had laughed at Spider because she couldn't hit the ball with the paddle. She had taken the toy to her room and banged it on the floor until it broke. It had felt good.

Simone was an intriguing girl with bobbed red hair and wireless glasses. She was dressed like a flapper and looked like someone from 1920s Paris. The poem she'd read had been a disturbing six-page opus about her demon mother, foreign lovers, blood and needles and knives. Spider had noticed her on the first day, but Simone always slunk out after class and never spoke to anyone.

They went to the student union building for coffee. Simone smoked a pack of Gauloises and talked poetry while Spider admired her. She was curious about living in the dorm and Spider invited her to see it. Simone walked down the hallways on Spider's floor with her nose in the air then poked her head in the TV lounge. The group of boys yelling over the soccer match on the screen stopped and stared. "Cretins," she sniffed. The boys didn't say anything back because Simone looked like a slightly unbalanced underwear model.

Simone lived on the top floor of an old character house in a neighbourhood close to downtown. She had relatives in Bordeaux and planned to get a degree or two on student loans, then renounce her citizenship and move to France for good. "It will be much more poetic to starve in French than in English," she said. She had already been in school for five years. Every semester she took the minimum course load and worked at the university library for a ridiculously huge union wage, since they were in the union. Her home was glamorous and filthy.

Unwashed ball gowns, crumbling cakes of face powder, dead flowers, a stained couch, dark purple walls and sequins everywhere, hidden like poppies. Her kitchen table was heaped with books and they drank white wine as Simone read random passages aloud. She stopped only to delicately polish her eyeglasses.

Spider pulled out a joint she'd bought from the deadhead on her floor. "I learned in Psychology class that redheads are more susceptible to pain," she said.

Simone looked over. "Life is defined by pain," she said. She could get away with saying things like that.

Spider began to visit Simone all the time. She read poems out loud by Baudelaire and Rimbaud. At first it irritated Spider and then she started to like it. Simone was truly moved by great works of art. She loved the epic and the opus, she loved the Irish, and tragic romance. Every day she looked like a different character. One day she wore a pillbox hat and ensemble, then the next she'd wear red leather pants and stiletto heels. There were fake diamond rings on her fingers. Everything ended up as pieces of her poems. She had a battered suitcase filled with dried flowers and a British lover with a crooked mouth. Once she killed a neighbour's dog. An accident she swore.

47

The bartender had a shaved head and tiny silver hoops in his ears. His name was Elwood and he was one of the few straight men who worked in the club. He saw Spider looking at him and sent a tiny kiss that went straight to her clit.

Two girls shot a game of pool. One had a pierced lip and a dog collar, the other "God is Dead" tattooed across her shoulders. Dog Collar grabbed the other girl and licked from the bottom of her throat to the tip of her nose. The watching eyes around the pool table glittered.

Spider ordered another drink and Elwood gave it to her for free. They made small talk for a while, then he told her to wait for him after work. "You're going home with a Jewish porn star," Simone said. During the rest of his shift Elwood polished glasses and ignored her. Spider tugged her skirt, made symmetrical water marks on the table with her empty glass.

Elwood lived in a loft above a trendy coffee shop a few blocks from the club. They fucked on his black satin sheets between cigarettes. Spider liked how dirty and horny he was in the dark room. The next day at school she couldn't get the songs Elwood had played out of her head. She looked at the girls in the bathroom, how they fussed over themselves in the mirror. Spider thought about Elwood and the things he had done to her all night. In her room she played industrial music obnoxiously loud.

A few nights later she went back to the club when Elwood was working. After waiting in line she ordered a beer. "How are you doing?" Spider asked.

Elwood put the bottle in front of her. "Four-twenty-five," he said. Another girl was standing at the side of the bar. She was short and had big eyes and a limp. Spider watched them flirt all night.

"She looks like an inbred royal," Simone said.

"It's okay," Spider said. "Forget him." It only stung for a little while.

Classes finished and finals were over. Simone got Spider a job in the university library. All she had to do was push a cart through the aisles, picking up misplaced books. The library was clean and quiet, and a good place for hangovers. The pay was so good Spider could afford rent all summer and also save money. She planned to get a student loan for the next school year. She started to look for places to live. It seemed every girl who needed a roommate wanted to be a fifth grade teacher.

Spider looked at a room in a cheap condo near a shopping mall. The woman became hysterical when she caught her smoking a cigarette in the tiny plot of backyard. Another woman had hung up pictures of puppies and kittens, right there in the living room.

Simone found Spider a room in a house with her friend Marcus, a math student who worked at the concession stand in the theatre where they watched free films. Marcus had long hair and smoked weed, and looked very much like an ugly hippie girl. His girlfriend, Allison, lived there too, an art major heavily involved in student politics. Spider developed an easy friendship with them in the shared kitchen.

Allison came from a small town on an island up north. "It has the highest rate of teen suicide in the country," she said proudly. Three of her friends had killed themselves in one year.

"I drank a lot in high school," Spider said. "There's not much else to do in a small town, except a lot of drugs."

"That seems to be a common coping mechanism," Allison agreed.

Allison talked a lot. She explained the delicate balances in the ecosystems, and human rights abuses in Latin America, about cosmetic testing on animals, and corruption in the government, right down to the student union. Spider was impressed—she had never met any kind of activist before. It troubled her that she'd never formed a social conscience.

There were faint acne scars on Allison's cheeks and she rubbed them when she talked. She was kind and vacant, always starting stories she'd forget to finish: plots of novels, true Elvis tales, diner escapades. Her eyes were grey and sometimes blue, teeth as white as Chiclets. Growing up her mother had always told her she was ugly and fat, and made her pick up crumbs from the kitchen table and eat them.

Allison said the girl who used to have Spider's room had fallen through the ice at Lake Wabaska over Christmas. She'd been trapped under the ice for almost eight minutes and they had to cut a new hole to get her out. Her body temperature had dropped three degrees. Since then she'd decided to devote her life to good works. Allison said she'd quit school and moved to Nicaragua to work with the nuns and street children.

48

It was Sunday night at the club. Spider sat at a table alone while Simone danced on a speaker. Simone had gotten serious about her Irish boyfriend, who was some kind of physics genius and wore a black overcoat, even in summer. Spider didn't see Simone much anymore.

She was restless. School was going to be a drag that semester; her Linguistics and Sociology classes were uninspiring at best. Spider looked around, bored. Elwood was flirting with yet another girl. She really had to admire his strategic indifference. Then she noticed a boy against the far wall. He was the most intense person in the room. He wasn't handsome, he was skinny and there was a lack of symmetry to his face until he smiled. Spider felt like a monkey in a plaid dress and figured there was no way he was looking at her. She wondered if she had black lipstick on her teeth and concentrated on lighting a match. She smoked a whole cigarette and refused to glance back over. Then the boy walked across the room and sat down in the chair beside her.

"I'm Andy," he said. "I wish you were my girlfriend."

Spider could tell right away from his confidence that Andy had a horse cock. He wore a black sleeveless shirt and a dragon tattoo twisted the length of his arm. Andy quoted James Joyce. It surprised her. He had black, spiked hair and straight teeth. His eyes were slivers of blue.

Andy said he'd tried going to college but dropped out after a few semesters. He had been a janitor, a waiter, meat packer, and delivery driver. He was a musician and a painter too. After the bar closed he invited Spider over to see some of his work. They walked all the way to his studio that was cold and reeked of paint. The only thing to sit on was his loft bed and a rickety chair by the hot plate.

Spider took her time looking at his canvases. There were a series of half-cow, half-cowboy figures in clown makeup. He asked what she thought about each one. Her Art History class came in handy. Andy was sharp and angled but moved lightly like a cat. He crept up on her, gave Spider looks that threw her off guard.

"So, how do you spend your time?" he asked.

Spider said, "I sit around and wait for the mail."

He laughed. "I bet there's something you left out."

Andy played Spider the demo tape from his band, Sküzzy, and proudly showed her a review in a local underground paper that called their lyrics "brilliant and sickening." They hadn't had a show in a while because the guitar player had a warrant on him and left town. Spider stretched out on the bed. There were books in stacks on the floor, weird art deco ashtrays and puddles of candle wax anchoring empty bottles. Andy said he loved good vodka. There was a crazy look in his eyes. They talked about foreign films and dead rock stars and his favourite psychedelics. Finally he turned off the lights.

Spider stayed all night and the next day in his studio. They drank a cheap bottle of wine in chipped glasses. They were hungry so Andy took her to a fancy restaurant where he knew the cook. It turned out it was his night off and the waiter was a jerk so they kept dropping the silverware on the floor, giggling. When the waiter threatened to call the cops Andy and Spider walked out. Spider flicked his carnation as they passed and said icily, "You were obviously a *damaged* child."

"Spider, the soft-spoken punk," Andy laughed. They held hands and walked through puddles in the moonlight.

"I'm in love," Spider told Simone. She'd only been seeing Andy a few weeks and already her feelings for him consumed her.

"Why?" Only Simone would ask that and make her think about it. It was because Andy had a sad, regal look that made her love him while he slept. He wore a black leather jacket and every time she looked at him her thoughts scattered. Andy knew all the signs of death and destructive elements; he dreamed in German but couldn't speak the language. His wealthy parents had treated him shabbily and he told her stories of ridicule at dinner parties in a quiet voice she couldn't bear. He'd started exploring the streets while still a young kid. Andy was skinny and intense and so intelligent it made him angry his thoughts couldn't come out fast enough.

He slept with his long limbs folded around her.

Andy lived in the studio because it was free. Sometimes he bussed tables at the club for drinks. He hustled his friends so he didn't have to work and could spend his time writing songs or painting. People took care of Andy. He could leave for an afternoon broke and come back fed, stoned, with a full pack of cigarettes and money in his pocket.

"Where are you going today?" Spider asked him. Every morning she hoped he'd stay longer.

"Ask me whatever you like," he said. "But make sure you really want the answer." Spider didn't say anything else. She was grateful that she mattered at all and deep down hated that about herself.

She watched Andy from the window as he crossed the highway between rows of slow-moving traffic, cigarette and a scowl. He walked down the street and turned the corner and then the day belonged to him.

49

It was early morning and Spider left Andy's studio, walked down the street with the Pixies in her earphones singing *and this i know his teeth as white as snow.* Past the concrete apartments at the end of the block looming ugly like always, but then a pigeon flew through the patch of sky between the roof and the clouds. It was just a bird, a scavenger, but it made her think *Wait a minute, I'm happy.* She checked her reflection in store windows and almost felt beautiful.

Later on Spider stood in the line-up at the coffee shop where Andy was supposed to meet her. The woman with a bullring and thin lips working the counter told a stalling customer, "They pay me to make coffee, not *think* for you, too." Spider blanked out at the chalked menu of lattes. Andy was late and she hadn't brought anything to read. She sat at a back table and practiced flicking her Zippo. She thought of the poem Simone had written about her called *Waiting for Andy.*

Spider moved to a table by the window and kept looking up and down the street. Andy was never around as much as she wanted. There was a pay phone downstairs at his studio that no one ever answered and the building was always locked. Spider knew he liked it that way. She finished two cups of coffee and went to the bathroom three times but once was just to check on her hair and since it hadn't improved she went home.

Andy didn't call Spider for three days and then one night he finally showed up at her house. For the first time she was angry. "I was finishing some songs," he said, standing forlornly at the door. "Aren't you glad to see me?"

He came in and they watched a vampire movie she'd rented.

Spider made some dinner and they went to her room. They started kissing and a ball of crazy energy made her stomach tingle and they rubbed and licked and sucked and moaned and fucked and fucked all night until the room got lighter and she wished time could stop right there, half-asleep when she said *I love you* and he said *I love you* back.

Spider woke up in the morning and listened to Andy breathe as she lay next to him. She stared at his long eyelashes and rubbed her palm against the whiskers on his chin. It scared her how much she loved Andy sometimes, like the world would empty of colour without him. The way his eyes and nose and mouth and chin came together made her heart seize. Sometimes when he pulled out of her there was a feeling of emptiness that had not been there before. Spider rolled over and forced herself to get up, because the only thing she had control over anymore was when she left.

Spider walked down the sidewalk as the early traffic began to start, alone on the streets with her grainy eyes and bruised cunt. Her legs and back ached. She was doing poorly in most of her classes that semester. It didn't matter to Spider; she smiled at her shoes and up at the sun and at men delivering fresh bakery bread. Andy had said she was the girl for him.

Work dragged by and she snuck looks at a book she saw on the shelf about how to find the right mate, the kind of book she and Simone would've made fun of but she checked the boxes: Considerate Lover, Emotionally Secure, Commitment to Personal Growth and then slipped the book back when no one was looking.

She met up with Simone for coffee, aware each time she mentioned Andy's name. At home she tried to clean a bit but didn't get past the penny jar knocked over three days before. Marcus and Allison were having a potluck for one of their hippie friends. Spider couldn't remember if it was for someone who was having a baby, or moving to an organic farm, or because they had just gotten out of jail for protesting a clearcut. She went to her room and thought about how she and Andy had stayed in bed and listened to old tapes the day they found out that their favourite guitar player was dead. He had been a hero to them and the bastards had finally ground him down. Allison knocked on Spider's door but she ignored her. She stayed in her room and waited for Andy to call.

Five days later he did. He said he'd been out of town. "Why didn't you tell me you were going?" As soon as she heard the sound of her voice she wished she hadn't asked him.

"Relaaax," Andy said and Spider felt defensive like he thought she was one of those possessive ex-girlfriends he complained about. She wanted to explain that no, she wasn't like that but had the sudden thought that maybe she was and quickly got off the phone.

Two weeks went by and Spider thought, *two whole weeks*. Some nights she unplugged the phone so she wouldn't be waiting for his call. She shuffled back and forth from work to class and when Simone said, "I never see you anymore," it was the worst thing to hear because Spider was already starting to feel like she didn't exist. She agreed to meet Simone later that night at the club.

The music was loud and it was hot and familiar and everyone seemed restless and desperate to get laid. A kid in a Misfits T-shirt smashed his head against the glass on the DJ booth. His friends roared, but then the boy started to wobble which made everyone laugh even more.

Spider had a few beers and danced and realized she hadn't

thought about Andy for almost an hour. It felt like progress. She turned around and right then saw him at a table behind her. Andy was with a girl, his arm slung over the back of her chair. She was stunning—short, bleached hair, curvaceous body, and an obvious attitude. Andy leaned into her and smiled. It looked like they had been there for a while. He saw Spider watching him and stopped smiling. She pushed through the crowd to the bathroom and sat in a stall. Her hands wouldn't stop shaking.

After a while Spider came out and looked for Simone. Andy stood by the DJ booth alone. She got a stamp and smoked a joint outside but then felt really fucked up and just kind of sad. Spider went back in but the music messed her up.

She found Simone and said, "I'm going home." A loser in deck shoes tried to talk to her on the way out but she just walked past him to the door. Andy was on the street with his friends and Spider turned in the other direction so he wouldn't think she was following him. "Hey," Andy yelled. Her body froze all the way through because she heard laughter, and was sure they were laughing at her.

Andy came over a few days later. He said the girl he'd been with was just an old friend. "Don't give up on me," he pleaded. The sky looked like rain; it was a good night to stay in. Spider didn't want to be alone.

Girls had always flirted with Andy and he ignored them to a point but used the language, and he had the features to do it. Like all boys he enjoyed an audience. Spider couldn't bear to see him unhappy. His love was an intense, cavernous thing and when she tried to understand it her feelings created a deep hole of exhaustion within her. The rules of Andy's underground world—the dress and speech and behaviour—were inflexible and intolerant.

A kind of superficiality existed in this that she could never applaud, yet wanted desperately to be a part of. It had taken six months to admit that really, his paintings weren't very good.

50

Sküzzy finally got a new guitarist and for the first time Spider watched Andy play a show. All his friends from the club came: the goth with vampire teeth; the cross-dresser and his androgynous girlfriend; Elwood and the speaker dancers; the guy with the tattooed face. The bleached blonde she had seen Andy with came in black latex pants and a see-through top. She danced in front of the stage and knew all the words to his songs. Spider tried not to sit with her arms folded and stare. She was the hottest girl in the bar.

Spider pointed her out. Simone looked at her. "That's Desiree," she said. "Andy's old girlfriend." She went on to tell her they'd gone out for years and Desiree had recently moved back to town. "She used to work here," Simone said. Spider knew he'd never gotten over her.

After the show Andy and Desiree stood close, talking. Her white-bleached hair shone under the lights. Finally Andy came over and sat with Spider. She tried to say something but couldn't.

"You know Spider, you have a look on your face sometimes that makes me feel like I'm a real piece of shit," he said. She watched him stare across the room. Desiree's beautiful body was wrapped around the guitar player.

dirtbags > 155

"Your words not mine."

What she'd been waiting for had finally happened. The bouncer kindly opened the door for Spider as she left. All the way home she sang in her head. Walking out on Andy felt a whole lot better than waiting for him to leave.

51

Spider's house had never been cleaner. She let Allison henna her hair. Simone brought over bottles of white wine. Andy kept phoning and Spider refused to answer his calls. She didn't need any extra time to think about him so she got another job delivering a free music paper. After awhile she started to help around the office. The paper was run by music nerds who were constantly getting laid despite having few interpersonal skills. In one issue there was a write-up on Sküzzy, with a photo. The paper had reviewed Andy's band quite poorly. "You guys don't like Sküzzy?" she asked.

"They can barely play their instruments!"

"And man, their songs are fucked up."

"I dated the singer," she said. "He broke my heart."

"Aaaaawwww."

"So I guess the best thing about Sküzzy is that they're a band with hot ex-girlfriends," Spider said. The boys in the office laughed loudly. She sat down and read the article again. It was a funny review that made her smirk. Then she remembered the nice things Andy had done. Spider still missed him. The next time Andy called she decided to pick up the phone.

He said, "It's not you, it's me." He was confused and didn't know what he wanted. He said, "You have to believe that I love you," and "You're such a special girl." He said, "You deserve someone better." He said all the good ones.

After her last exam Spider planned to catch a bus home early the next day. Johnny had moved to Calgary six months before to work on the oil sands and was going to come home for a ski holiday. Spider couldn't wait. It had been a long time since she'd seen her brother. He'd called once to tell her his plans and make sure she was going to be there, too.

"I'm going to offer a prayer to Ashera for your safe passage," Allison said as Spider packed. "She was known to the Semites as the Queen of Heaven." Allison had gotten a little too into her Eastern Religion course. More often Spider was beginning to think that higher education was just a racket run by bureaucracy and elitists. The world of academia was too small and dry for any real individuality to flourish. The life most of Spider's classmates wanted meant nothing to her—marriage, house payments, struggling careers as sitcom writers and teachers. The idea of her own children had always unsettled her.

The phone rang. "Merry Christmas," Andy said. He asked if he could come over. Allison left Spider's room in disgust. In the morning he helped with her duffel bag and walked her to the bus depot. It occurred to Spider that men were always helping her pack her things so she could leave them.

52

Spider called long distance. Andy finally had a phone. They talked late at night, about books and stories and the moment that everything led up to. They talked about anything but what was between them. She could see Andy in the city so clearly. The small town in the mountains always felt like winter. She asked about his cat, Meesha. Spider wondered if she still slept on his bed.

Sometimes Spider thought it would have been better to have things end with screamed insults, a slammed car door and squealing tires. She wrote long, rambling letters to Andy describing the hicks in town. Short, cryptic letters with no punctuation. She found aerial photos of the pulp mill. They sold three for a dollar.

Andy told Spider stories about people she didn't know. Tragedies were shortened to anecdotes which were briefly amusing but never enough to fill an entire conversation. She resented the good-natured tone in his voice, how contented and happy he sounded without her. She tried not to call late at night, in case he wasn't home.

Finally Johnny's car pulled into the driveway, a few days before Christmas. It was good to see him. He looked strong and healthy, with the same freckles and easy smile. They drove up to the ski hill and looked down over the town. He rolled a hash joint and Spider told him about Andy. She said, "It hurts to be in love." They had a good laugh about that one. Johnny asked about their parents and she shrugged. It didn't seem like anything they could say to each other would be worth opening up their feelings in the small space of the car.

She asked about his job on the oil patch laying pipe. "I've saved a lot of money," Johnny said. His hands were hard and cracked. "I want to buy a houseboat," he said. "I've been thinking about heading down to Florida, maybe start looking at boats."

"I'm jealous," Spider said, but she wasn't. Johnny said she could come down and visit. They shared a cigarette and talked about nothing important—fishing, alligators, *Miami Vice*, superior Canadian beer, riptides. Then they didn't talk and that was what she loved about Johnny, it felt easy and comfortable not saying anything at all.

"It's good to see you," he smiled. "Little sister." He looked out over the mountain. In the light from the dashboard Spider could see the little league pitcher he used to be in the bones of his face.

They began to make their way back to town. "I'm going to see if Tucker's around," he said. "I'll drop you off at home." It was snowing and difficult to see. A truck zoomed up the hill too close to their lane. Johnny swerved and fish-tailed, and then the car began to slide. It was black ice, the most dangerous thing on the mountain roads. The embankment came closer. All Spider said was "Johnny?"

They hit the side of the road and began to fall through a deep dark space. The car flipped and there were sounds of bending metal and snapping branches. The windshield shattered. Spider screamed as they rolled over and over. Her cheekbone came down hard on the gearshift.

She knew nothing more.

53

Spider's mother stood beside her hospital bed with her hand locked over her mouth. Spider's left arm was bound with thick white bandages, an IV was taped to her hand and another came out the side of her neck. She was so numb the ends of her fingers tingled as if her blood carried tiny knives.

The hospital smelled like laundry, egg farts, and antiseptic. Spider's nerves were alive with shocks that ran up and down her body. It felt like she would never be able to sleep again.

"Where's Johnny?" she croaked. Her mother twisted and wrung her hands.

"He's in surgery," she said. "You're okay. You fractured your cheekbone and your arm is broken. But you're going to be just fine." And then her mother began to sob. It came from deep inside her somewhere, and it was the worst sound Spider had ever heard. Her heart stretched to the point of snapping.

Spider's father stepped up and put his arm around her mother. "Johnny's vertebrae were crushed," he said. "The doctors are trying not to amputate his legs, but…" Spider closed her eyes and listened to the soft hiss of machines around her. She went back to the last few minutes in the car, she cursed and begged and bartered with God to please make her brother okay.

"Your brother's conscious," a nurse said, shaking her awake. "You can go in and see him now. He's on a morphine pump and he's pretty doped up." The doctor had just informed Johnny that he'd been paralyzed. He would need his family near.

The nurse wheeled her down the hallway with her IV. She

heard Johnny shouting. "Leave me here," Spider told the nurse, and parked in the doorway of his room. The doctor stood beside his bed.

"YOU'D BETTER GET OUT OF MY WAY," Johnny hollered.

"Why?" the doctor asked calmly.

"Cause I'm going to jump out that window and float down to my car and drive out of here!"

"John," the doctor began. "The morphine will cause—"

"I'M GONNA JUMP OUT THAT WINDOW AND DRIVE MY CHEVY OUT OF HERE!" Johnny sobbed. "GET OUT OF MY WAY!"

There was nothing to salvage below his waist. The doctor said that even though his legs didn't have to be amputated, he would never walk again. Spider lay in bed and thought of all the things that had been taken away from him. He would never ski again, or drive his car. He would have to sit in a wheelchair for the rest of his life.

All she had was a broken arm and a black bruise across her face. The profound unfairness of that, how her brother should suffer while she walked away from the accident was almost unbearable. She wished for a broken neck, a snapped spine. The sickness took over and she rang the nurse for a shot. Then Spider wept into the pillow until she finally fell asleep.

The dream went on and on.

Spider walked through a mansion, into a giant carnival of rooms. Each one was different; some were gold-tiled and filled with sparklers, some were covered in rich purple velvet, others set up for parties with presents and balloons. The rooms were full of people Spider knew: Jenny White and Amy Flowers, Auntie Marlene and her little cousins. In another room her grandfather played cards at a smoke-filled table with a group of men who roared with laughter.

And then Johnny was beside her. They walked on together into rooms that were empty and cold and Spider was afraid but Johnny held her hand. Her eyes began to close in a heavy sleep but Spider wanted to stay with him. Johnny put his arms around her.

He said, "I'll be there to walk you home."

Spider woke up with a gasp. Her mother leaned over, touching her face. Spider saw that her eyes were red and her mouth looked raw.

"There was a blood clot in his leg," she said.

Johnny was dead.

54

It's wrong what they say, that life keeps going on. When Johnny died the days were cold and dark. Nothing moved.

There was memory, blurred: the hospital, the doctor, white pills with crosses. A church. The car ride to the graveyard. Uncomfortable relatives in the kitchen. Johnny's friends crammed on the porch, Tucker in an ill-fitting suit. There had been a write-up about Johnny in the newspaper, and one of his old girlfriends read it aloud until her sobbing became too much and someone else took over.

Spider went and stood quietly next to her father. After awhile she took his hand. She realized that for most of her life they had ignored each other. Her father had gone back and forth to work, rarely speaking. Nothing had ever seemed to upset or excite him and Spider had never known if it was because he had invested too deeply in their lives or too little. She thought of the fun times with her father when she and Johnny were little, how he'd taken them to the pool for family swims and threw them off his shoulders. Sometimes he played catch in the backyard. He knew everything about the woods. He took her brother hunting. They killed gophers, grouse, deer, elk, and moose. Spider was a girl so he never took her.

Spider felt a deep and terrible pain for her father that day. He'd worked in the plant for twenty-five years. Her mother was often unhappy. There was never extra money and he hated to buy on credit. He had buried his only son. It had been a hard life.

"I always told him that he drove too fast," Spider's mother said. She refused to let anyone see her cry.

"He was used to driving on the flatlands," Spider said. "He'd forgotten the curves."

"It was that damn car!"

Wheels meant movement, and to Johnny movement was everything. "What's wrong with you," Spider cried. "Why do you always need something to *blame*?"

Her mother slapped her face, hard. Her father stepped in between them. "Who do you think you are? Oh," her mother told her, "you're just like the rest."

Uncle Nick began to talk about a lawsuit. Spider's mother was held captive by her sisters in the kitchen. Her aunts smelled like they were rotting from the inside out. Spider's father moved on to rye whisky. She sat with the remains of her family and realized she was alone.

Every so often Spider felt a sudden panic, a sense of losing or forgetting something very important. Then there would be a sickening thud in her stomach when she realized it was because Johnny was dead.

She knew that feeling would never go away.

55

Spider's broken arm mended and her fractured cheek healed itself. She looked the same. By the time the frozen containers of food from the neighbours were gone and the dishes returned, her mother had settled into a joyless routine. Watching TV, washing already clean floors, the endless chopping of vegetables. Her father went back to work night shift. The house was quiet like a tomb. Spider tried to help out in the kitchen; she tried to talk to her mother. Her father went to the scrap yard and saw the remains of Johnny's Chevy. When he came back he sat down beside Spider on the couch. "Don't blame yourself," he said.

"I don't."

He squeezed her arm. "Life is short," he said. "Don't rush through it."

"Okay Dad," she said.

Johnny's room had long since been packed up and put away but Spider liked to lie on the mattress. For hours she just stared at the ceiling.

"Please get out of there," her mother finally said.

A month went by and then another. Simone sent a postcard from Paris. Spider didn't tell anyone from school about the accident. Allison sent her boxes and Spider's mother mailed her a cheque. She called a few times but Spider didn't phone back. She missed the deadline for next term and didn't see how it mattered. She knew she would never go back.

Spider's mother thought she should get a job at Wal-Mart. "Or Super-Value," she said. "Cashiers make a good wage." They ate dinner in front of the television. Her father was like a ghost.

Spider stayed in bed longer and longer. The days quietly crept past.

One night she called Andy. She could not tell if she missed him. Her life before Johnny died seemed only half-remembered. "Hello?" he answered. "Who's this?"

"It's Spider," she said. The distance echoed through the phone lines; the connection was unusually bad.

"Spider," he said. "It's been awhile."

"Andy," she said, her voice cracking. Then she heard a girl's voice in the background. It was one o'clock in the morning.

"This is a really bad time," he said. Spider could tell he wanted to get off the phone. "Can I possibly call you back?"

The sound of the dial tone seemed to fill the whole room.

Spring began. Spider's mother talked about her crocuses. She talked about her garden and jams. It got too hard to listen so Spider stopped trying.

Dave Newton called long distance. He'd been working up north tracking caribou and his father had told him about Johnny over the radio phone. It was good to hear Dave's voice. It made Spider remember the swimming hole and the drive-in, and the whole long summer when they had been in love and her brother was still alive.

She moved from the bed to the couch. Beneath her skin the bones felt sharp. Spider slept during the day and watched movies all night. When her father got home from work in the morning, she went to bed. Whole days passed without speaking.

The television reminded her of all she didn't have: good times, a tan, party invitations, a boyfriend, lunch dates with the girls, a secret admirer or best friend. A brother. She went for a walk but her sense of unease just turned to mild panic. Everything was pointless, senseless, and sickening. Spider ate, read books, got herself off, and stayed in bed as long as she could. Sometimes she lay on the backyard grass under a tree and stared at the sky through the leaves.

One afternoon after she'd woken up she went outside and stood on the front porch. The street smelled like traffic and gas and cooking meat. Every morning the rest of the world woke up and went on living. She scraped her knuckles against the stucco until they split and bled. Her brother was dead.

56

The phone rang one night and it was the loudest sound Spider had heard in weeks. "I'll bet you have no idea who this is," a man's voice said. He sounded familiar.

"No."

"It's Billy Newton."

"Billy," she said. They hadn't spoken since the prom. "How are you?"

"Doin' okay. Uh, I need to meet you."

She started to feel anxious that Billy was going to bring up Johnny. "Billy, it's not—"

"I won't be here long," he said. "And I have something for you." Spider agreed to meet outside the arcade later that night.

Billy had cut his hair and had a tattoo of a dagger on his neck. He leaned against a red Firebird out front. "I can't believe how big you've gotten," she said. "Jesus, that sounded stupid." Billy looked at her strangely. She knew what was coming next.

"I heard about the accident," he said. "Sorry about your brother. He seemed like a decent guy."

"He was," Spider swallowed. "He was a really nice guy." Her chest got tight and she bit her tongue hard between her teeth. She didn't know how to lock her feelings down so she just said, not very nicely, "What do you *want*, Billy?"

He opened the trunk and took out a black knapsack. "Get into the car," he said. In the front seat he showed her it was full of tightly packed bags of pot.

"Dave told me to give that to you. It's sixteen ounces of weed." He zipped the bag shut. Spider looked at him blankly. "It's a fucking pound," he said.

"I don't smoke that much weed, man." She tried to process why Dave would send her a suitcase of weed.

"Do whatever you want with it," Billy said. "Sell it. He said you might need some money. You always seemed like a pretty resourceful girl."

"How did Dave get this?"

"Let's just say he funds a side business." Billy unrolled his window and spit.

"I don't know what to say," Spider said. "I mean, thanks."

"Thank Dave," Billy said. "He said he'd never met a girl who could roll a joint like you."

It was late and they drove out to the lake. Spider knew she would fuck Billy Newton that night. He told her how hurt he'd been when she'd started dating his brother. "You ditched me at the prom," she said. "What'd you expect?"

"Dustin's fucking car broke down!"

Spider shrugged. "I didn't know that."

Billy slammed the steering wheel with his fist. Then he turned toward her. "I've liked you for so long," he pleaded. He kissed her neck and she let him. She wanted something other than the dull pain of grief inside her. It could have been anyone's cock. The fact that it was Dave's brother was an unfortunate coincidence but Spider didn't care. His hands shook as he pulled down his jeans. She crawled into the back seat on top of him.

When it was over Spider buttoned her shirt and told Billy, "This is never going to happen again." They didn't talk on the ride home. When he pulled up to her house he unrolled the window to spit again. She got out with the knapsack. Billy squealed the tires as he drove away.

Spider went into the house and washed off his smell. Then she slept better than she had in a long, long time.

The next day Spider borrowed the car and drove slowly up to the ski hill. She parked and lit a cigarette, her mind filled with thoughts. The road atlas lay open on the seat beside her. She looked at it for a long time.

Vancouver. The name sounded like the coolness of water over rocks. Spider had always wanted to live near the ocean. A plan began to work itself out in her mind. There was a lot she would leave behind.

Spider's mother drove her to the bus depot early one morning. She had made a call to her sister Clara in North Vancouver and insisted Spider sleep in her extra room until she found a place to stay. The bus pulled out onto the road and the driver began to recite the safety precautions. Spider looked back at where her mother was parked. She took her hand off the steering wheel and gave a small wave.

It was too much for Spider, to know the terrible burden it was to love, how it could break and possess you. Nothing would hurt that much ever again. She knew she was alone, and it was the most powerful thing she could feel. When she got to Vancouver her life stretched as wide as the city skyline.

She was twenty-one and had no love for anyone.

dirtbags > 169

PART THREE:

Spider Songs

57

It was quiet on her parent's front porch. An angry dog barked somewhere down the road. Spider looked at her ripped jeans and played with the broken bracelet from Otis she'd fixed with wire. The hills surrounded the town in a blanket of green—cedar, pine, fir, birch, spruce. Spider could see one single house, right up in the middle of the forest, the red roof and curl of smoke from the chimney. She started to write about it in a letter to Sally and Blue, but things lost their meaning when she tried to write them down.

Her father had developed a low, rattling cough. Spider was ashamed she'd stayed away so long. It had been over two years since she'd moved to Vancouver, but it seemed so much longer. Her parents were easier with each other now, like something silent and deep was understood between them. The house had been oiled and disinfected, and the basement completely redone. Her parents had more money and empty rooms where their kids used to be.

It was hard, but sitting on the front porch Spider tried to look at her life. Falling in love with Otis was like a joke that had gone too far. She thought about living in the House of Cock when the love had begun to run out. How they'd sat on the couch and watched their lives become smaller; bills unpaid, teeth that couldn't get fixed, whole days spent hungry, rolling butts from the ashtray. But none of that mattered the nights Otis came to bed. Her spine felt hollow and there was a hotness in her throat when they'd loved, slipping into the same half-dream together.

The weeks passed. There were three meals a day and a comfortable bed, clean laundry, and hot tea with cream. Spider was grateful her mother let her sleep late, remembering how she used to stomp outside her bedroom door weekend mornings. "Get UP," she'd yell. "Teenage girls do not need to sleep all day unless they were doing things they shouldn't have been the night before!" Spider giggled to herself and stayed under the covers.

She knew her mother had worked hard. Shopping, cooking, constant rounds of scrubbing. She baked bread once a week and did laundry every second day. When she had a spare moment to relax it seemed so foreign she couldn't just sit and enjoy it. Sometimes as a child Spider had watched her mother across the room because she looked so pretty lost in thought while ironing a shirt or rolling dough. Then she'd get an overdue bill, or realize the garbage hadn't been taken out, and all the noise would start up again.

Spider wished she could tell her mother about Sally Pepper and Blue; how the three of them had always been out looking for good times. When it seemed the city was full of punks like them counting their pennies to get high. They'd wanted their drinks and their pleasure, to speed up and not move on. And love, they had sworn it meant nothing.

We really used to believe that, Spider thought. Amazed.

One night after dinner Spider sat with her parents, quietly watching television. The program was an investigative report about the growing drug use between teenagers and young adults, how much younger children were becoming addicted.

"It's a damn waste," her father said.

Her mother clucked her tongue. "Why would those kids do that to themselves?" She seemed genuinely upset and confused.

"I can tell you why," Spider said. Her mother looked at her with alarm. "It's because being artificially happy for a few hours is better than not being happy at all."

"Oh now," her mother said.

Spider went out to sit on the porch. She loved her parents and knew they loved her, but they would never make sense of each other. It was the silence of the mountains that Spider understood, like the rare stillness on a Sunday morning, those quiet times she and Candace had clung to when their boyfriends had dragged their weary bodies to lie beside them, a raggedy bunch of kids just trying to find their way. The walk home from the corner had always seemed to take forever when Spider knew Otis would be there.

That night she dreamed of Vancouver, and Otis, and needles that fell out of the sky. Spider woke up and the past came down on her hard. There was too much she had left unfinished.

She had to get back to the city.

58

A week later Spider knocked on the front door of the House of Cock. A taxi waited in the driveway for her. Frank came to the door. "Otis isn't here," he said.

Spider didn't say a word to him and walked into the house. There was nothing left of Otis in the room they'd shared. The good pots were hers and Spider found a box on the back porch. She thought of the times she'd sat listening to the neighbourhood, how Otis played air guitar when cars with loud stereos drove past. The backyard was covered in pine needles that smelled like Spider's hometown. A couple of old towels on the clothesline flapped stiffly. They'd been hanging there for months.

The good times of summer had long ago faded in the kitchen. "I don't know where he is," Frank said. "He came back from the hospital with his dad and left again." Frank leaned against the doorframe so heavily it sounded like it would collapse. Someone downstairs turned up the stereo and he stomped on the floor. They thumped back.

She continued to pack her dishes without saying anything. Frank watched her and after a few long minutes finally went into the living room. He turned on the amp and played a song on the guitar, and when it was finished he started all over again. Spider recognized it—Otis had written it for her as a birthday present when he'd had no money. Frank played the same chords over and over, loud and merciless.

Spider left through the back door and walked around the house. She got into the taxi and as it pulled away from the curb Frank came out onto the porch, yelling from the front steps.

The driver looked over at her and Spider rolled up the window. "Don't stop," she told him. "Just keep driving."

Spider went to visit Sally, who was now bartending in a restaurant pub in Gastown. Sally was the happiest person she'd seen in a long time. She ran out from behind the bar and spun Spider around in a circle. "You're back!" Then she pulled out a stool for Spider and poured two celebratory shots, which they immediately followed with two more. "You fuckin' little bitch! I didn't hear from you once."

Spider considered. "I tried."

"I missed you."

"I missed you, too. How's Blue?" Sally told her that Blue was still with Sid and that he'd practically moved in. "I'd like to see her," Spider said. Sally went to use the phone and when she came back she said that Blue would be over in a while.

"Blue finished her GED and started taking classes at community college. Of course she's aced every assignment and is totally obnoxious about it." They had a good laugh at that one.

After a few drinks Blue finally showed up. She sauntered in the restaurant and gave Spider a casual kiss on the cheek like she could barely muster the energy. Spider's heart sank. She'd seen Blue drive away people before. One day she'd stop looking at them, or laughing at their jokes. Pretty soon she wouldn't answer when they spoke and she'd ignore them in front of other people. Blue could make anyone invisible to her. Spider knew there was a part of Blue that enjoyed the power.

"Sally told me you're acing your college classes."

"Just chemistry and physics."

"I always knew you were a smart girl."

"That's right," Blue said. "I'm not wasting anymore time fucking around." She looked pointedly at Spider. "Make any sense to you?"

"Yeah," Spider said. "Sure."

There was an awkward silence which Sally filled by pouring another round. "Are you coming over to our place? You can stay with us, right Blue?"

Blue did not answer for a moment then she said, "Yes." But she was not looking at Spider.

"Thanks," Spider said. "I really mean it."

Blue continued on. "The thing is, I've spent most of my life partying and you know what? I don't remember half of it. I don't want to be the wasted party girl anymore. For so long I wanted to have a normal life and make dinners and have a job but I could never do it because I was a *drunk*."

She reminded Spider again that she'd borrowed money from her months ago and it hadn't been paid back. Spider thought of her picture that Blue had tacked right to the wall in the bathroom after she'd first moved in, how eventually the colours had started to bleed. She doubted it was still there.

"How was it visiting your parents?" Sally asked. "Did anything interesting happen?"

"Once I got chased by a pack of wild dogs." She was relieved to see Sally smile.

"What are you going to do now, Spider?"

"Get a job. I don't know, learn Spanish. Find a hobby. Sleep all day and party all night."

"Christ," Blue muttered. "I think I need a shot of tequila." Sally pulled a bottle off the shelf. "And that better be the good shit!"

The taxi steered easily through traffic on the way home. Spider had waited as long as she could and asked, "Have you guys seen Otis?" Blue looked over her shoulder at Sally from the front seat then told the driver to turn the radio louder.

"Listen," Sally said. "I heard that Otis quit doing drugs. The heart attack or whatever freaked him out so much his father put him in rehab."

"I never met his dad."

"Well, Otis supposedly went straight."

"Have you seen him?"

Sally shook her head. "He hasn't been around."

"I need a favour," Spider said.

Sally made a few phone calls. It took a while but she tracked down where Otis was living and got his number. "Are you sure about this?' she asked, holding out a piece of paper. "Think of what you're holding onto, Spider. Maybe you just want to let it go."

"It's not that easy," she said.

"Yes," Sally said. "It is."

59

Spider walked into the coffee shop to meet Otis. He sat in the last booth, back against the wall. Otis got up and they hugged each other. They stood like that for a long time, while the people in the restaurant walked around them.

"I heard you left town," Otis said. He looked good. His hair was cut short and his arms were huge.

"Yeah. I couldn't stay. My head was too messed up."

"I got a job on the docks. Can you believe I get up every morning at six o'clock and go to work?" Otis said he had a dog named Tiger. He looked healthy and happy. Spider knew him well enough to tell he had another girl.

"I met someone," he said. "I'm sorry." Spider put more sugar in her coffee and stared at the spoon.

"I'm sorry I split," she said. "I waited until they told me you were okay."

"You probably saved my life," he said. "Spider..."

"Did you meet her in rehab?"

"She's been good for me," Otis said. "I wanted to get straight for a long time."

dirtbags > 179

Spider twisted her hands under the table. "Otis, why couldn't you get straight with me?"

There was a look of fear and bewilderment and loss on his face that she knew only the two of them could understand.

"You never asked," he said.

Spider stayed awake for a long time that night, until the combination of tears and codeine finally lulled her to sleep.

They'd taken everything so lightly.

60

Spider knew it was her last days with Sally and Blue.

She tried to get her old job back at the bookstore, but Ralph had hired another girl. Spider couldn't blame him—she'd never given notice before she left, just shown up and asked for her final paycheque which he'd quietly given her. Spider searched for a job but there were few prospects and the city had become very bleak. A conservative government was forcing everyone to live with a bit less and now that was what they expected. Spider had some money from her parents but it was running out fast, and it was becoming clear that Blue didn't want her around. Spider had never felt so hopeless. So many things had changed.

There was fried banana in the fridge and expensive flowers in a vase on the low wooden table. But still there was Sally, sitting in the window, swinging her long, strong legs. She leaned over and passed the joint to Spider. "Hey, remember the time you put a spoonful of hash oil in your mouth and your teeth got stuck together? HAH HAH!" Spider would miss Sally Pepper more than Blue, with her black bobbed hair, perfect tits, and mean streak she tried to control. She thought of Blue as a girl more New York than most New Yorkers. Blue made a lot of money at the restaurant and she wore it very well. Her weekly manicure made her nails gleam like tiny rubies.

It was raining, again. Blue and Sid were fighting. When Sid left Spider knew Blue was going to take it out on her and she was right. Blue stared at her across the living room, smoking ominously. "You know Spider, I once thought of you as my little sister."

"Thanks."

"I was *horrified* you could live in the House of Cock. It was so dirty and harsh. I knew all along that Otis was on the pipe and you were smoking that shit, too."

"Yeah."

"Why were you doing that?"

Spider thought for a moment. "Because it made me feel like I might die," she answered. "And sometimes I enjoyed that."

"Jesus, Spider. You're the most destructive girl I've ever met."

"Self-delusion is the largest part of happiness."

"What?"

"Voltaire."

Spider looked at Blue's face and knew every once in a while she could still surprise her.

Sally had apologized then told Spider that she'd have to sleep on the couch because Sid was storing his gear in the closet room.

Sid went back and forth to the Island to visit his small son and ex-girlfriend who had a new husband. He wasn't sure if he would go back tree planting again that year. Blue told him, "You know I'm against it!"

Spider searched the want ads and made frantic phone calls. Sally said she needed to relax and took her down to the restaurant where Blue worked. During the evening it featured live music. Tara was there and like usual was trying too hard. Blue called her a plain girl told one too many times she was pretty. Carlos, who worked bar back, laughed and spun—the only person on the tiny dance floor. At Lulu's Grill the owner, a large Ecuadorian man who did ecstasy each Friday night, sat at the bar and gurgled. The waitresses all made thousands of dollars in tips every month and were paid less than minimum wage. Sally got up grinning and pulled some dance moves with Carlos. Sally's lifeline was long. That night Spider stayed awake and listened to the mice in the walls creep quiet as death.

It was Blue's day off. She wore an orange tank top with a fringed red skirt and looked like she was on fire.

She told Spider she had an invitation to the West End to see Joe the bartender's one-man show. Spider knew Blue would catch every train and bus with ease. She was impossible to stop some days. Spider woke up at seven a.m. when Blue got home the next morning. They sat together listening to the garbage truck outside. A man and woman screamed at each other on the street. The woman yelled, "YOU lost my child!"

Blue was still drunk and happy. Before she passed out she gave Spider a hug. "Get your life together," she said. It made Spider feel good because Blue hardly ever did that anymore.

It was Friday night, and Spider decided to see a band. She put on tight pants and safety glasses for street-prowling, wishing somehow she could rewrite the weeks of terror and Vancouver rain. In the mountains, if she listened to the silence, at least one tiny piece of the world made sense. But Spider knew the city had wedged itself inside her.

Here there were so many beds, but few places to rest.

61

For the first time, Spider applied for welfare. Sally warned her she wouldn't be able to get a cheque because she didn't have an address. They were fixed with the landlord and he wouldn't add her name to the lease. Spider was nervous to go to the office and asked Sally to come with her. It was in a grey room in a grey building with a sign that said, "No Needles" on the bathroom door. Spider stood in line and watched a girl in the corner crying. Everyone else seemed pissed off. Spider had waited two weeks to get a case worker who had lifeless eyes and looked like a fat tree frog.

"You do not qualify for assistance," the woman bleated from behind the bulletproof glass. "You quit your previous job therefore making you ineligible."

"Why can't I get a welfare cheque?"

"You have no home address or proof of residency."

"I quit my job because I was going through a hard time," Spider said. It felt like the line-up was pressed against her back. "I just need some emergency help to get back on my feet again."

The woman looked at Spider as if she'd just said the stupidest thing she'd ever heard.

"Fill out these forms." She gave Spider a card that said she had an appointment in two weeks. "You will need to see an intake worker."

"I just waited two weeks!"

"It's the earliest available appointment," the woman informed her.

"But I can't—"

"At that time an officer will review your case and decide if there is a possibility of assistance."

Spider lost it. She slammed her fist on the counter and screamed, "I'M ASKING FOR SOME FUCKING HELP YOU CUNT!" Security walked her out.

Out on the sidewalk Spider cried with gulping sobs. Sally rubbed her back as they sat on the bus bench. Spider's hands shook as she lit a smoke.

"Sally, I'm fucked," she sniffled. "I can't get a cheque. I've got no money, no job, nowhere to live. I can't keep staying on your couch."

"*I* would never kick you onto the street, Spider. But I don't know what Blue is going to say about it."

Spider's shoulders slumped even further. As she smoked she took stock of what she had: some connections, her pussy, a whole lot of semi-friends who liked to party. She'd been disappointed so many times that when the cigarette was over she finally lost the sad look on her face.

It was impossible to know how far she'd go.

62

Billy Newton lived out on the furthest edge of the suburbs. Spider hadn't seen him since he'd given her the pound of weed. Once he'd left a message saying he'd moved to town and Spider had written his number down but never called him back. It was a long drive to his house. Sid was nice enough to lend Spider his van. Billy had told her to make sure she parked in the back.

He opened the door with the same look he always had when Spider saw him, like he wanted to cry, smack her, and fuck all at the same time. The place was lit up, but he didn't mention a grow show so she didn't ask. The living room and kitchen were empty except for an old couch and a long table with benches covered with plastic. A skinny woman with greying-black hair sat on one side of the table and a tall, balding man stood beside her.

Billy told Spider to wait and went down the hall. The house was freezing. Spider walked over and sat down at the table. The man left and the woman began to tell her how she had lived in India and worked with child beggars. When the man came back he had a large rolled cigarette in his hand. The woman stopped talking.

A stranger with dark hair shaved close to his skull walked into the room. His sharp black eyes looked at them. He left without speaking. The woman began to tell a story of how in India she'd caught malaria from the dirty street urchins.

Billy called for Spider to come to his room so she went down the hall. He sat on the edge of the bed and lit a cigarette. "What's going on, Spider?"

"Listen Billy, I'm fucked right now. I really need to make some money."

"I don't have any weed for you, Spider."

dirtbags > 185

"I'm a smart girl. Are you sure there's nothing I can do?"

"No."

"Billy, please."

Billy took a long drag of his cigarette. Then he opened a drawer and pulled out a large white rock of cocaine, vacuum-sealed in plastic. "I'll give you this half-ounce for three-fifty."

Spider stared at Billy and said nothing. Billy shoved the coke back into the paper bag in his hand. They looked at each other. "Let's do some rails," he said. Billy dumped some powder on the dresser. Then he locked the bedroom door.

Spider bent over and did one fat line, then another. It was good stuff and she got high, real fast. The room became hotter and she got so sweaty she didn't care and when she bent over the dresser to do another line Billy put his hand under her skirt and between her legs. She stayed bent that way as he pulled her panties down. Billy's fingers made her wet. He unzipped his jeans and she felt him against her ass. Spider tried to get another line up her nose as he ground into her. And then she wanted to be fucked, she wanted to be fucked by Billy Newton more than anything she'd ever wanted. She remembered the people in the kitchen but couldn't stop moaning. When he was finished Spider used his T-shirt off the floor to wipe herself and got dressed. The brown paper bag went into her purse.

Driving home with the windows open, sore and cold, Spider knew the first person she was going to call.

Otis.

63

As soon as Spider paid off her debt to Blue, she told them she was checking out apartments and wouldn't be there much longer. When Sally asked her where the money was coming from Spider said she was doing odd jobs.

"What kind of work is it?"

"I help out this...*handicapped* man." Spider wasn't a very good liar so Sally backed off. "Okay," Sally said. "If you're doing something that you can't tell me about, then I'm sure you have a good reason."

"Believe me. This guy is crippled."

"Hey, it's dropped," Sally said, and Spider knew it would stay that way, which is why she loved her.

Spider generally kept pretty strange hours. She and Blue didn't talk much anymore. When Spider moved out she knew they were all relieved.

And that really broke her heart.

64

Spider moved into an old rooming house divided into apartments. A man lived in the basement and tried to sell his paintings to the lawyer and functioning junkie upstairs. The landlord was an old rummy named Mary who seemed to be overly fond of single girls. There was a view of North Vancouver from Spider's big kitchen window but the living room was the size of a stamp. Spider fixed it up with little rugs and coloured lights. She hung up plastic stars and strings of beads. The apartment was full of plants she and Sally had stolen from hotel lobbies during drunken refurbishing missions.

As Spider swept the dirt into corners she listened to Iris, an old lady two houses down, yell at her big new TV. There was a steady stream of kids through her door and Iris yelled at them, too. Her nephews stood on the front steps all evening, checking out cars and the passing women. It was a Vietnamese neighbourhood and the white hookers were all hard-looking. With each joint Spider settled more into her new home.

There was a palm-reader downstairs from Spider with a sign in her window that said, "Magickal Jasmine." Underneath it read, "A Telephone to the Dead." It made Sally Pepper chortle when Spider pointed it out. They were carrying a set of wooden shelves that Sally had grabbed for Spider from the alley. They heard Jasmine's door open. She was an elderly lady with long grey hair. "You're the new neighbour," she said, shuffling outside. "Will you please see me for a reading?"

"Can my friend come, too?"

"Of course."

They left the shelves in the hallway. Inside Jasmine's dim apartment they sat at a round table covered in silky white cloth. Jasmine excused herself for a moment.

Sally leaned forward and whispered, "What do you think, Spider?"

"I figure it's a way for an old woman to sniff out her neighbours."

"Speaking of sniff, did you get a whiff of this place?"

A strange odour emanated through Jasmine's apartment, not exactly unpleasant but hard to describe. Every nook was crammed: corked bottles, old books, candles, containers of herbs. Spider half-expected Jasmine to come back in a purple robe and pull on some weird headgear made out of tinfoil. Instead she sat down and gently took Spider's hands, inspected her palms. Then Jasmine closed her eyes. After awhile she began to make a humming sound, like her throat was vibrating.

Spider concentrated on the cheap gold rings Magikal Jasmine wore on each finger. She was reminded of the years she'd spent shoplifting, how the same jewellery had slipped easily out of the display case and onto her fingers, sometimes before she even knew she was going to steal.

Then Jasmine leaned forward and whispered, "*There is wind.*" Her voice became louder. Spider felt the hair on the back of her neck stand up. "*Wind and glass and sky. The air. The air is fire.*" Jasmine clutched at Spider so hard her knuckles were white.

Sally stood up and pulled Spider's arm. "All right, we're done here!"

Jasmine's hands fell to the table. Her eyes opened and she said, "Would you dears like some chamomile tea?"

"No!"

"No, thank-you," Spider said. "Some other time." She and Sally went outside and kept walking around the block holding hands, trying to laugh it off but they couldn't.

65

Sally Pepper's friend Jonas had been busted by Immigration for being in Canada illegally and was going back to Denmark. He'd decided to take nothing with him and gave the girls the keys to his apartment. He hated his landlord and didn't want to leave him anything of value. Blue, Sally and Spider drove over in Sid's van.

"How do you get busted by Canadian Immigration? I mean, you'd have to be *really* stupid to let that happen," said Blue.

"These rich playboys kill me," Sally said. "All Jonas cared about was that he left the landlord only garbage." Once inside Spider called dibs on the couch, bed frame, and kitchen table. Blue took the computer and stereo and Sally claimed the big screen TV. They divided up the movie and music collection. Spider and Sally both wanted the coffee grinder. It was an excellent appliance for busting up weed. They took his food, curtains, electric toothbrush, condoms.

Spider found a camera on a shelf in the closet. It seemed new and expensive. "I'm going to learn how to use this."

Blue said, "I'd like a camera too."

"Spider found it," Sally interjected.

"I'm taking it," Spider said. Blue backed down. They could tell from the look on Spider's face that she meant it.

Spider visited Ralph at the bookstore and he gave her a bunch of photography books. He also told her he had a friend named Stanley who sold jazz records through his used bookstore and might be able to give her a part-time job. Ralph said he would call her. Spider read through the books and manuals and then went to a camera shop and got fixed up with batteries and film. She began to take photos of what she saw around her neighbourhood; graffiti, street signs, garbage, alleys, overpasses. There was a whole disturbing series of road kill and then the houses where her old boyfriends used to live. Spider was hired to work a few days a week in Stanley's store, even though she'd never listened to jazz. When she got her first paycheque she bought a new lens for the camera and took it with her everywhere.

Sally made some calls. Sally was good like that. It turned out her friend Rodrigo knew someone who had been a semi-famous model thirty years earlier and was now a respected photographer. She needed an assistant for a day-long photo shoot. Spider waited in a coffee shop early one morning. Twenty minutes after the designated time an older woman walked in. She wore a wool coat, dark glasses, and a hat pulled low. There was a certain way she walked, with her legs opened wide and a low-shouldered stride that exuded supreme confidence. "You're Spider," she said, before dropping into the seat across the booth from her.

"You're Jean."

The young waitress came over, smiling. "Coffee," Jean barked. The waitress fled. Jean turned back to Spider. "Do you know anything about photography?"

"I know the basics." It didn't seem smart to lie to this woman. "I'm barely a dilettante. I just learned how to roll my own film."

"Then you will simply do what I tell you."

"Of course!"

"It will involve adjusting the lights. Holding my camera. Waiting."

Spider needed the money. "I can definitely do that," she said. Jean's lips twitched slightly when the nervous waitress poured her coffee.

"Rodrigo said I would like you."

"How do you know him?"

Jean told her he had been her tour guide in Costa Rica, and she'd sponsored him and his family to come to Canada. Jean had lived all over the world. She had a flat in Paris, a son who didn't know her and an ex-husband in New York she despised. Jean described her ex-husband in terms of fecal matter as they walked to her house. She owned a place on the lower eastside where she spent the rainy part of the year.

There was nothing in the house except a heavy wooden table and an elaborately carved wooden chair, a divan and a white-sheeted bed on the floor. Throughout the day a succession of down-trodden artists posed for a shot that would be put in a calendar and sold by a local charity. Each left with a bag of groceries, and the promise that Jean would give them a portrait. Jean's professionalism impressed Spider; she treated people with a certain dignity that elevated everyone around her. At the end of the day Jean made a pot of tea and they relaxed in the kitchen. She talked to Spider about photographing caribou, the works of Knut Hamsun, the Squamish Five, Nan Goldin, her view in Paris of the Seine. Jean had a streak of silver in her hair and Spider guessed she had never been lonely a moment in her life.

"Thanks for the letting me work with you," Spider said. "I learned more today than I would have from an entire photography course." It was true and Spider didn't think Jean would mind the compliment. Jean said she would make an exception to her rule, and allow Spider in the darkroom as she developed the prints, too.

Spider made a copy of her favourite photograph for Sally and Blue. It was a shot of a giant puddle reflecting the street lights and neon. It made Spider think how after a storm the salt air carried over the train yards and the grimy streets of Chinatown, until the smell of rain and the ocean came right up to the window. How for a little while it seemed like the whole stinking city was clean.

"I love it," Sally said when she saw Spider's photo. "I can't wait to frame it on the wall." Even Blue was impressed. Spider told them it was because she'd found something she really liked to do that was better than boys or drugs or sex, how there was nothing else like it in the world.

And then she met Eddie.

66

The people in the bar annoyed Spider. They seemed like old posers and shallow kids who only cared about haircuts and the trendy brand of sneakers. The spilled beer that ran across the bar floor was like the lies that connected them all. Sally had dragged them out to see a band named Green Meat she really liked. "The last guy I fucked from this bar," Blue said, "had balls that smelled like rotting cabbage."

"I saw Green Meat here once with Speed Beaver," Sally beamed and raised her glass. "It was an excellent show. I'm so glad they're playing here again!"

Spider said, "I've never seen them."

"Their live show kicks ASS."

Spider went to the beer line. The crowd was getting rowdy and some crusty punk rammed into her. A large man walked over and shoved him back. Spider looked up at him like the last thing she wanted was to be in the middle of a brawl between two monsters. The crusty staggered away. She said, "This drink line-up is like a war machine!"

The man put out his hand and introduced himself, smiling. "I'm Eddie," he said. Next to hers his hand was the size of a catcher's mitt. She gave him a sweet-faced smile. "My name is Spider."

"Spider?"

"Actually, it's Spider Rose."

"Spider Rose…"

"It's my real name," she said. "Honestly."

"My god," Eddie said. "That's just about the cutest thing I've ever heard. You're adorable." Just then Blue came over. Her hair was raspberry and she looked like she had been in a bad mood for most of her life. Eddie said, "Hey Spider, do you smoke weed?"

Spider said, "Sometimes." Blue rolled her eyes at that. Eddie and Spider went out the back door. He told her that earlier some random guy had shoved a joint in his pocket for which he was very grateful. Spider sparked it up and he said, "So, what do you do?"

She said she moved around her house, getting stoned in different rooms. Eddie said, "I like to travel, too."

"This is nice weed," Spider said.

"Did you come here tonight with your friends?"

"Yeah. I've never seen this band, but my friend Sally Pepper is a big fan."

"She sounds like a cool girl."

Spider described how she and Sally had once lived together and worked out an elaborate bartering system with a network of dirtbags to stay drunk everyday. Spider said, "It had seemed so hellish sometimes and now I wish it could be that easy."

They heard the guys tuning up onstage. Eddie said, "Damn, I have to go in."

"Why?"

"Well, I'm in the band. I play guitar."

"Oh yeah? What's *that* like?"

Eddie told her about Baldo the bass player, who had a bumpy head, and Crank, the drummer, an ex-speed bag who had gotten fat when he'd quit and talked non-stop in a squeaky voice. They were good guys and he liked being on the road with them, but said the novelty wore off real fast.

"No way," Spider said. "I've never been anywhere. How can it get boring to constantly be in new places?"

"It's like this," Eddie said. "You pull into a town and leave the next day. Usually you have to sleep in the van with a bunch of stinky dudes, and someone's always sick. It can be depressing. Constantly driving. Crap towns and hostile crowds. Promoters rip you off or shows get canceled and you don't get paid. You can't keep a job or a girlfriend. All your pets die. Then there's the worst feeling of all, that when you're finally back in town no one cares." They heard someone scream into the microphone for him and Eddie apologized. "It's been really nice talking to you," he said, and bolted.

Spider's eyes followed Eddie as he left. She liked his face. He had a beat-up look like he knew life was going to keep dealing him an unfair hand but it wasn't going to get him down.

Back at the table Blue sat with her arms folded. Spider told them, "I just smoked a joint with the guitar player." It impressed Sally to no end. Green Meat started to play. People yelled out song requests: "Penis Avocado!" and "East Van Enema!" Girls lifted up their shirts and shook their tits, while a rough crowd jerked at the front of the stage. Eddie's fingers flew over his guitar like the devil had given him black magic. Sally and Spider danced together in the crowd then Spider hopped her way up front and pushed into the pit of thrashing boys. She went down fast. Eddie saw her and hollered from the stage. Sally pushed her way into the crowd to pick her up. Spider had a crumpled look on her face and when she raised her fist everybody cheered.

Green Meat played their classics: "Stacey is a Douchebag" and "I've Got a Crush on a Crackhead." Spider and Sally rocked out a little more gently in the corner. The set was almost finished when Eddie played a few chords into the next song then stopped and stepped to the microphone. "This is a song for a girl named Spider Rose," Eddie said to the crowd and looked right at her. Then he played a jagged, cheery riff. The kids went wild. Spider watched him for a moment then grabbed her jacket and split. Sally chased her out.

"What's going on?" Sally asked when she caught up. Blue fell in behind her. "You didn't want to stick around and talk to Eddie?"

"I thought that band really stunk," Blue said.

Spider didn't answer. She had decided she was through with boys—the love they gave was always too much or never enough. All the good times would turn into what hurt most when it finally ended.

The next day Sally brought over some cassettes to play for Spider, and filled her in on the history of Green Meat. They were a respected band who'd never let any type of success change them or their music, and always put on an energetic live show. Sally was a long-time fan. She asked Spider if she thought she'd see Eddie Camaro again.

Spider shrugged and said, "I don't care."
She wondered if Sally Pepper believed her.

67

Crispy Jones started a band. They hadn't even known Crispy was a drummer, and were shocked when they found out he could also play the saxophone and slide trombone. His band was called Kiko and the Bones. The singer was a short Japanese girl with very bad teeth. It was a benefit show and Sally convinced Spider to go and take pictures of Crispy's band. When Spider got there she found out his band was first on a bill with Titmouse and Green Meat.

Spider had barely been out since the last Green Meat show. Jean had given her an extra key to her darkroom which Spider cleaned in exchange for its use. It felt natural to Spider how huge waves of time could pass in the glow of the red light and the heavy smell of chemicals, radio low in the background. Sometimes she couldn't afford her rent or the electricity got turned off and Spider had to scramble for money. She rolled up her pennies for cigarette money and lived on loaves of day-old bread and hot sauce.

Blue refused to go to the show since she and Crispy were fighting. He owed Blue twenty bucks he wouldn't re-pay, saying she borrowed his skateboard and gave it back with stress cracks and she swore they'd been there before. From what Spider had heard, Blue was in a foul mood because lately things were off again with Sid. When Blue had a boyfriend she expected flowers and dinners out and expensive gifts on major holidays. Sid was an aspiring sous-chef, and could do none of those things.

Spider took a few shots of Crispy in the corner with Sally as the band set up their equipment. Eddie tapped her on the shoulder and when Spider turned around he held out a Heineken. He said, "If I'd known you were coming I would've put you on the guest list!" His teeth really busted out of that smile.

She introduced Eddie to Sally Pepper who tried to contain herself. "I FUCKING LOVE YOU GUYS! Oops, sorry," she said.

Eddie invited Spider and Sally to sit at his table with Crank, the fat drummer. Crank was clearly lurking in the back to check out the chicks in the bar. Eddie and the girls ignored him. Spider had dyed her hair so the tips and the bangs were bright orange. "That looks really cute," Eddie said, touching a lock of her hair. "You're like Halloween," he said. "And Chrrrrristmas."

Sally looked at Spider who made it impossible to tell what she was thinking. Spider pulled out her camera and pointed it at Crank. He flipped her the bird.

"That's a pretty big finger."

"Pull it," Crank said. "It'll smell like pepperoni."

"When I eat pot brownies my farts smell like weed," Sally said.

"Bullshit! Your ass smells like some guy's cock!"

"Fuck you!"

"Oh, Crank," Spider said. "I'd love to know what your parents were like."

He said his dad had been a country musician and was now in prison. "Oh yeah," he added as an afterthought, "and my mom is a junkie bitch." He waddled off to get more pre-show drinks. Then the band started and Sally, Spider, and Eddie went up front to watch Kiko and the Bones. They were horrible. When they finished Eddie went to go talk to the soundman.

Spider didn't see Eddie during Titmouse. She tried not to

think of how much she liked his crooked teeth and faded blue tattoos, his spiked hair and mean black eyebrows with those pretty eyes beneath them.

Once Green Meat started to play Spider found a spot to photograph from the side of the stage. Eddie threw her a shout-out and waved. He later told Spider when he'd realized she was ignoring him it made him like her even more. The show turned out not to be very good. The singer was so wasted he forgot the words and took a swing at Baldo that missed and he went flying off the stage. After it ended and the crowd began to thin out Eddie loomed over Spider like a friendly sweating giant. He invited her and Sally for a round of drinks on the band's bar tab.

"He's really got a crush on you," Sally whispered. Eddie kept looking over and smiling as he loaded out the gear. They could hear Crank, drunk and screaming at anyone he could. Eddie came back to the table with band shirts for Spider. Sally went to talk to Crispy. Spider had another drink with Eddie, who said he was happy that for once no one was giving him a hassle after the show.

"Are you a photographer, Spider?"

"I work in a bookstore."

"Have you read Kubalowski?"

"I love Kubalowski. He's the most relevant writer of the past fifty years!"

"I found a limited edition print of *Mad Dogs in Heat* at a used bookstore in Sacramento."

"I cannot fucking believe that."

"Listen, I gotta take a leak," Eddie said. "Wait here, I'll be right back." When he left to go to the bathroom Spider grabbed her camera bag then hurried down the stairs outside. Eddie caught up to her and said, "Hey, where are you going?"

Spider just shrugged and didn't say anything so he took her

hand. "I don't care if you take off," he said. "As long as you come back again." Spider just looked at him. She didn't answer but she didn't drop his hand either, and they went back inside together.

68

Eddie Camaro had grown up with his parents and older sister, Maxine. Maxine kept running away. His mother became more and more religious and none of them could stand her. Eddie got used to his sister not being around.

Maxine would go for weeks or months at a time. She first ran away when she was thirteen after she'd got caught shoplifting a dog collar from Safeway. She split to Toronto with some guy and a few months later she came back. Her hair was cut short and she was really skinny. She didn't look very good. When Eddie's dad opened the door he started to cry. All Maxine said was, "Can I sleep?" She was out for three days straight. Two months later she left again. That went on for a couple of years. Once Eddie and his father picked her up in Montreal where she was living in a dirty basement and shooting up coke. Then she married some guy in the army and moved to Halifax. Eddie and his dad never saw her again.

When Eddie was fifteen his mother divorced his father and married a widower from her church. Sometimes she made Eddie stay with her new family out in the suburbs. He started getting into trouble for breaking into people's cars and stealing bikes so his stepfather paid to send him to private school. As Eddie was already big they put him on the junior football team. He actually enjoyed playing. He began to do well in school until one day a group of guys from the team drove by in a car and yelled, "Punk faggot!" They threw a bunch of eggs at him. Somehow he caught one without breaking it and pelted it back, right in their window. One of them got out of the car swinging and Eddie broke his jaw with his fist. It had been a great day.

Eddie was sent back to public school. He was a smart kid who figured out early that the system was bullshit and wanted no part of it. For Christmas his dad bought him a cheap, knock-off Gibson. After that all Eddie cared about were girls and music and getting high. He didn't graduate because he almost never went to school, and at the age of eighteen decided to move across the country with his buddy.

When Eddie first came to Vancouver he got a job as a waiter in a West End restaurant and kept falling in love with lesbians. After work he'd sit up playing guitar with the other coked-up waiters. Sometimes he worked as a bouncer and for years he was a roadie on and off for different bands. He played guitar in a bunch of groups that never went anywhere: Muckraker, Bono Has Mono, Smudge. Then he was asked to join Green Meat. The singer had been in the legendary band T.U.R.D. Eddie went on the *Deathbed Blowjob* tour across North America and Europe. Green Meat was on the road for eight months straight. They wrote another album and went on tour again. It became the only kind of life he knew.

69

Spider was in the bottom of her closet, searching for a black Lycra tank-top she believed she'd once owned, when the phone rang. "I'll get it," Sally hollered. "It's for yooooou," she said, bringing the phone down the hall and handing it to her. Spider immediately knew it was a boy.

"Hello?"

"Hey, Spider. It's Eddie."

"Oh. Hello Eddie."

"What are you doing?"

"Not too much." Sally began to jump up and down and Spider, who was still sitting in the bottom of the closet, threw a shoe at her kneecap.

"I wanted to invite you over to my house for dinner."

"When?"

"How about tonight?"

"Oh, I don't know—"

"I figured it would take some convincing before you'd agree."

"Oh yeah?"

"I've even done my laundry."

"Hmmm."

"And I can make you anything you want to eat. I'm a really good cook. Fucking amazing, really." Spider told him that he sounded like a true ladies man but, in spite of that, she'd come over.

They met on the corner and walked down the street for groceries. Spider wore jeans, motorcycle boots, and a white undershirt. Her long hair was shiny and smelled like coconut shampoo. The combination of what she looked like and what she said melted Eddie's brain. She forgot to buy cigarettes and they went back to the store. She seemed even smaller than Eddie remembered as she stood beside him. Spider wore sunglasses and put two packs of gum in her pocket while she talked to the old Chinese grocer. Outside Eddie said, "I love you tiny chicks."

Eddie lived in a nice, clean apartment on the top floor with a big balcony. Spider was impressed that there were even extra rolls of toilet paper in the can. They smoked a joint on the balcony before dinner. "This view of North Vancouver is the same from my place," she said. "The lights look like they're eating their way up the mountain."

Eddie poured her another glass of wine. "I'm going all the way tonight," he said. "I even got the good wine, the kind with a cork and not a screw top." Eddie had made whisky chicken and mango chutney. Spider was impressed. After dinner they drank more on the balcony and talked. Eddie asked what her life was like growing up.

Spider was solemn for a moment. "I had a brother named Johnny," she said.

Spider walked into Eddie's room and sat on the edge of the bed. He knelt in front of her and gently took off her boots. Spider was drunk and roared, "Let's fuck!" Eddie seemed like she'd almost hurt his feelings.

Later that night Spider had a bad dream. She woke up scared until she felt Eddie there. He put his hands on her face and kissed her forehead. After he'd fallen back asleep she crept out of bed and dressed in the darkness.

It was a long walk home. The streets were shiny in the moonlight and there were old parts of summer everywhere.

Eddie left a message for her that she didn't return for a week. Then she called him and went over to his place again. The next morning he made pancakes while she smoked a joint and watched a documentary about African killer bees. Eddie casually mentioned Green Meat were driving down to Portland to play with Stink Fish, and invited her to come. She declined. During a commercial she asked if he knew a guy named Otis Renfrew.

"Yeah," he said. "From the House of Cock."

"You know it?"

"Sure."

"You know Frank?"

Eddie said, "I know Frank's an asshole, and one day he's going to piss off the wrong person."

Spider thought, *There's a lot he'll find out one day.*

70

Sally had enrolled in beauty school after she'd read an article that said cosmetology was the fastest growing business in British Columbia. Spider sat at Sally's kitchen table, letting her tweeze her eyebrows for practice. Sally filled her in on the recent gossip: Blue and Sid were back on again, and he'd gotten a job in an expensive kitchen so now she was talking about marriage. Bigfoot had come back to town and Sally hung out with him sometimes. Angel was having a baby with Jude the Dirtbag.

Spider told Sally about Eddie and his invitation to Portland. "Ow! Goddamn it, this hurts!"

"Sorry," Sally said. "That's why *I* never do it."

"Anyway, I'm not going to go, obviously."

"Why not?"

"Because the reason Eddie and I get along is that we don't see each other that often."

"Yeah, but going on tour with a band sounds like such a great time!" Just as she finished saying this, Blue came into the kitchen.

"I talked to a girl at school who knows the bass player," she said. "She told me the boys in Green Meat always have a room nearby so they can do their drugs before the set. Dating a rock star doesn't seem like a good idea for a girl who's trying to clean up her life."

Spider sighed. "So some of the guys in Green Meat do drugs and get drunk before a show. Big fucking deal. As I recall you used to party *yourself*, Blue. And I'm not even dating this guy."

"Damn," Sally interrupted. "Tara has the curling iron. I'll be right back."

As soon as the front door clicked shut Blue said, "What is it with you? I mean, look at what happened with Otis."

"Yeah, that's really great that you can bring up my ex-boyfriend and throw him back in my face for me."

"It wasn't just with Otis."

"What exactly is the point here?"

"Look, just because we've grown apart doesn't mean I don't worry about you. You burn a spliff and don't care about your problems, but that doesn't mean they don't exist, *dude*."

"Now I'm getting hassled about smoking weed? Are you crazy? Sally Pepper smokes weed!"

dirtbags > 205

"Sally doesn't have a joint in her mouth every second of the day."

"How much weed I smoke is none of your business."

"I just think it takes a lot more courage not to hide from reality."

Spider had known Blue for a long time, and found that pretty much laughable. "Ding!" Spider said, getting up. "I'm done."

"Hey," Sally said, coming in the apartment as Spider was leaving. "We're not finished. Why are you leaving?"

"Let her go," Blue said. Spider slammed the door and kicked the wall in the hallway.

"FUCK YOU BLUE," she screamed.

71

Green Meat was going on tour for two months to support their new album *Teenage Moustache*. The kick-off show in Vancouver with the Black Mallows was sold out. Eddie put Spider on the guest list, along with Sally. Security pushed back the line at the door and the bouncer shit-kicked some guy down the steps. He seemed to really enjoy doing it. Eddie told the doorman holding the guest list, "Me and my girl." Sally caught Spider smiling into her hand. Backstage Eddie introduced the girls to everyone. Spider was trying to quit smoking. She had herbal cigarettes that smelled like horse manure, which she would light then immediately put out in disgust. The entire set Spider go-go danced at the side of the stage where the audience couldn't see her.

Crank passed out beers after the show to all the girls backstage. Spider avoided hovering near Eddie. It was a trick used before; she'd dodge the boy until she got her feelings locked down, watch him from the edge of the crowd until she knew what was going on. Large and scary-looking men pounded on Eddie's back like they were his oldest friends. Every time Spider spoke Eddie bent down to listen as if everything she said was important.

Eddie asked Spider to feed his pet snake while he was away. He said, "A girl named Spider can't say no to taking care of a snake. And since you'll have its life in your hands, and my house keys, you can't just disappear."

"Eddie, I'm not good with snakes."

"I'll pay you fifty bucks a week to take care him. It eats a frozen baby rat once every fourteen days. You don't have to take it for walks or anything. If you want, you could even stay here while I'm gone."

"I have my own apartment."

"Yeah, but it's not in a safe neighbourhood. And I've got cable TV."

"All right, I'll come and feed the goddamn boa constrictor while you're away. But I'm not touching it."

"It's okay. You can touch my other snake," he leered.

Spider leered right back.

After he left, every few days Spider went over to Eddie's. She enjoyed his porn collection, his stocked cupboards, and watching movies on the enormous TV. Sally came over sometimes, too. Sid was back in town and she couldn't go through another night of having to listen to him and Blue grunt in the bedroom. Spider invited Sally to sleep over at Eddie's with her and have a movie night. "Great," Sally said. "It'll give them a chance to fuck in the living room."

They looked through Eddie's records and books and Sally petted his snake. "Someone left it at the house where Eddie was living, so he ended up keeping him," Spider informed her.

"A boa constrictor named Salazar is a hideous thing," Sally said. Spider agreed with her. Salazar was four years old and Eddie said when he died he was going to take him to a taxidermist to stuff. Spider showed Sally a sliding panel at the bottom of Salazar's aquarium where Eddie used to keep his drugs. "Sneaky fucker," Spider said. Eddie had also left Spider an ounce of weed with a note that said, "For taking care of Sal."

They got stoned and watched movies, eating junk food and giggling until their stomachs hurt. Spider gave Sally Eddie's bed and fell asleep on the couch. In the morning they woke up early. Sally rolled a joint and they smoked it on Eddie's balcony, enjoying a bit of sun and staring at the mountains. It was Spider's favourite time of the day, because the greyness softened the city in the morning. She didn't have her camera, but pointed out to Sally what a good photo it would be, the rusted truck roofs on the street they saw looking down from the balcony.

72

When Eddie got home he opened the door and saw that Spider had fallen asleep in her underwear on the living room floor in front of the television. When he gently woke her up she screamed. "Oh god," she said. "I was up late watching a horror movie festival. That scared the hell out of me."

"I couldn't think of coming home to a better sight."

Spider smiled lopsidedly as she hurried to the bathroom. Eddie sprawled out on the couch. When Spider came out she was dressed and put on her shoes. Eddie looked puzzled. "Do you have to go somewhere?"

Spider said, "I figured maybe you'd like to be alone. Since you just got back to town and everything," she added.

It intrigued and infuriated Eddie that he could never figure out why she'd need to leave. He asked, "Are one of those talks coming?" but Spider didn't say anything else. Eddie said, "Look, I really missed you. I thought about you all the time. Didn't you miss me too, Spider?"

She said nothing for a moment and then she smiled. "Only every day," she said. Eddie got up and hugged her and she hugged him back real tight.

73

Crank had a white Christmas party at his house. He encouraged everyone to do cocaine, that way if the turkey was dry no one would care. Even Blue decided to go. It turned into a really big party: dancing girls, little gangs of crusty punks, even some dude in a Mexican wrestling mask. Spider looked beautiful in a turquoise frock. There was a big rip in her black nylons. She liked the feeling of getting trashed in a nice dress.

Spider sat with Sally and Blue in the corner with their drinks, feeling sentimental. They talked about when she'd first moved in with them. Sally said, "Here's to the good old days."

"When we thought we had all that time to waste," said Blue.

Spider told them she wanted to put a book of photography together and call it *The Long, Drunk Summer.* Someone tried to take one of Crank's beers from the fridge and Crank karate-chopped his arm. Baldo and Tara began slow-dancing, despite the fast, loud music.

Blue pointed out Otis across the room, talking to someone outside the bathroom. He was thin and seemed agitated. "It doesn't look like Otis is straight anymore," Sally said.

"When people get straight they get on what they call in AA, 'the pink cloud.' They feel all this bliss and enlightenment," Blue said matter-of-factly. "Well, not only is Otis off the pink cloud, he looks like he's been snorting it, too!"

Otis saw Spider and came over with a dry-lipped grin. Spider stared at him. Whenever Spider knew she would see Otis she made sure she looked good. As much as she fought it, something in her stomach always hurt.

"Hey Spider," he said.

"Hey Otis."

Otis said, "You holding?"

"I can't help you Otis," Spider said.

"C'mon, Spider," he begged. "Just gimme one line."

Spider tried to walk away but Otis followed her. Sally Pepper grabbed his arm to hold him back. Spider hurried out onto the patio, even though it was a freezing December night and she didn't have a jacket.

She lit a cigarette and looked out into the ugliest time of year. Johnny had died right before Christmas. After they'd returned home from the hospital the presents stayed wrapped under the tree for weeks. The pine needles turned brown and fell on the carpet. One day Spider had finally sat down and opened the boxes. A bathrobe. A video tape. Chocolates. Gloves. After that she'd piled the presents in the corner for Goodwill and her father had taken the tree to the dump. No one had said a word about it.

Spider went back inside. "Come on, Otis," she said.

There was a jam session going on in the living room. Otis and Spider finished snorting coke in the bathroom. When she came out Eddie winked at her across the kitchen. He was drunk and said, "Spider, you're a good woman." The look on her face was like she'd won the lottery. It seemed to irritate the hell out of Blue.

She followed Spider out to the patio. The cold wasn't bothering Spider any more. "Ahhhh," she said. "Blue, I love how there's always people partying somewhere like it's a Friday night."

"It *is* Friday night."

"Right!"

"So you started selling drugs to Otis." The look of pleasure immediately dropped from Spider's face.

"No, I didn't. All I ever did was to call him and say, 'Hey, who's going hard tonight?'"

"Well, now look at him." Otis and Sally were in a heated conversation in the corner. In truth Otis got a shiny look in his eyes whenever he talked about coke and everyone had known it wouldn't be long before he was partying again. "Spider, is this really what you want out of life?"

"I don't know. Sometimes I think that if I could go back in time to when I was a kid, and then fast-forwarded to see myself in the future, I'd be pretty disappointed."

"This is what I'm talking about," Blue said, and Spider began to tune her out. "...I mean, Fergus Finn? Oh yes, foam mesh and a moustache, how *original*! Total garbage dick. Otis Renfrew—

what the fuck? That guy was so lazy he was scared of sudden movement…"

Spider was grateful for the distraction when she heard Sally's voice begin to rise. Sally turned to walk away from Otis and then he said something else and she spun back around with a raised fist. "She just punched that creep right in the nose," Blue said with wonder. For a second Spider thought, *Oh, that is fucking beautiful.*

And then she turned and ran.

74

Spider tried to stay away but Eddie woke up one night and she was there. Before he even turned on the light he knew Spider was on the edge of his bed. Her hair was wet and there were black circles under her eyes. She told Eddie she'd kept her key. She wouldn't tell him why she was crying.

It was because of many things—the sad boys and the dope and the House of Cock and Otis. Spider crawled on top and kissed Eddie open-mouthed. Her lips were warm and wet. There wasn't enough air to breathe between them. His cock felt hard like a rocket and Spider rode him, shooting stars.

Afterward she lay there with a look of sadness and loathing on her face that made Eddie think she would leave again. He told Spider he loved her and wanted her to stay. She curled her hand across her mouth and wouldn't say anything at all.

75

Jean came back from Paris. Spider had arranged to show her some of the photographs she'd taken. It was intimidating. Spider braced herself for what Jean would say, and had spent hours in the darkroom trying to perfectly develop her favourite shots: a hippie girl smiling with her feet on the dashboard of a van; Crispy and his pregnant girlfriend sleeping; the crazy-eyed man who prowled her alley; an overweight woman in an ugly red hat. Jean lingered over the print of Sally and Blue in their underwear, pushing each other for space at the bathroom mirror.

"This is very good," Jean said. "Yes. You have talent. Keep working on your portfolio. Absolutely do not stop."

"It's too late to stop. The world seems easier to manage through the filter of my camera."

Spider decided to print another copy of Blue and Sally's picture and drop it off to them on the way home. When she finally left the darkroom it was late and she could hear the cars on the wet street outside. The rain made everything empty and gleaming. It brought back how the sound of tires on wet asphalt had comforted her when she'd first come to Vancouver and made her feel less alone. Back then the city had seemed magical and without memory, but that was a long time ago.

Often she had cut through strange neighbourhoods and looked in windows from the street, just wondering what all those different lives were like. Smelling their food cooking, listening to their conversations, making judgments about them by the TV programs they watched. It was a game she'd played for hours when she'd lived at Aunt Clara's, getting off the bus and walking until her legs ached. Inside those houses she'd seen whole lives. All that regret and misery, right there in the window.

As she walked her thoughts went back to Otis. She'd spent long, lonely months trying to pinpoint the exact hour, the moment he'd stopped loving her. Soon she'd moved on to the others—Andy and Fergus—trying to figure out why it had gone wrong. Then she'd started paying attention to the news: the ice caps were melting, sea levels rising, storms getting stronger, species disappearing and introducing new diseases. It was depressing as hell, so she went back to crying over Otis. When she'd finally wrung it all out she discovered hardness in her chest that felt like a weapon. But then Eddie came and played the songs that made the coldness in her bones go away.

Eddie had piled up his gear by the door, ready to be loaded. Green Meat was driving to Austin to record the songs they had written for their next album, *Touchin' My Gennies*, and planned some tour dates on the way back to Vancouver. Eddie would be gone for nearly two months. Spider was propped on the floor against his duffel bag. He said, "Will you come down and visit me in Texas?"

She just lay there, turning the pages of the comic real slow, not reading it. Finally she looked up. "I don't want to go to Texas," she said.

"How about meeting me somewhere on tour? Or you could drive down in the van with us."

"That sounds like a groupie."

"Nah, we call them barnacles. You can't get rid of those. You're different. I can't seem to make you stay."

"Heh-heh."

"Bring your camera," Eddie said slyly. "You'd get some killer shots. And it would be fun to take a road trip. Baldo's bringing *his* girlfriend. Come with me right now."

"I have to work in three days," she said, but they both knew Stanley was nothing if not a laid-back boss. All those jazz records had really mellowed him out.

"I'll fly you home whenever you want to go."

The van pulled up and honked outside. Spider reached out her arms and Eddie picked her all the way up off the floor, and she squeezed her legs around his waist. "Jesus, you've got a sweet little ass."

She kissed him and the van honked again. "We'll stop at your place so you can pack a bag," he said. It felt like it had been a long time since she'd done something spontaneous. Spider looked at the front door.

76

It was going to be a long ride, but already Spider loved driving down the highway in Crank's '84 Chevy van. There was a bunk built into the back and one above the front seats. The singer had flown ahead. He had an ex-wife, and a new one he cheated on, and girlfriends in every town.

Spider shared the van with Eddie, Crank, Baldo, and in a horrible twist, Baldo's new girlfriend, Tara. Tara now had short brown hair and her make-up made her blue eyes seem even smaller. Baldo had been dating her two weeks. She sprawled across the back bunk with her feet on the ceiling, crossing and uncrossing her fake-tanned legs.

Eddie drove and Spider sat in the front seat. He smiled over and said, "Hey pretty lady." He snapped his fingers to the music and Spider asked him what was playing. "It's Ella Fitzgerald," he said. "I used to live with a girl and we were so broke all we had in our apartment was a bed, cassette player, and that tape. We drank cheap wine and sang along for entertainment."

"What happened to her?"

"She got religion and move to Kenya to be a missionary." Spider told him she'd grown up on Judas Priest and Iron Maiden and knew almost every song. He laughed when she blew three perfect smoke rings in a row and said, "Spider, you're the coolest girl I know."

The van was stocked with cases of beer. Crank liked the way the empty bottles sounded when they smashed on the highway. Because of this it surprised Spider when Crank informed her that he'd graduated from Concordia University with a Political Science degree. He relived his all-night debates of whisky shots and fat rails; pounding knives into the wall to threaten his roommates; research missions for bubble hash or opium or peyote or liquid acid or absinthe or speed. Spider herself fondly recalled how she used to stay up all night writing passionate, drug-fueled papers hours before they were due, and had gotten the best grades of her life. At the time he'd had a girlfriend in Women's Studies and they would drunkenly shout quantum theory at each other, scream lines of free verse out the window stoned at three a.m. Spider began to reformulate her opinion of Crank as a meathead. She asked if he'd learned to speak French in Montreal. "Yeah," he said. "RIBBIT."

Spider gazed out the window and smoked a Marlboro while Crank described how his feminist girlfriend really knew her way around a cock. Tara and Baldo began to make out in the back bunk. There was no line uncrossed; they were friends in the most fleeting and dangerous way.

They stopped for the night and sat crowded at the back table of a bar in a town named by Indians. "I've lost my brightest season," Tara wailed. It was almost her twenty-sixth birthday. The boys listened for a moment then rolled their eyes and went to play pool. Spider stayed at the table with her and chain-smoked. Tara said, "Spider, you're a pretty girl and maybe you've hadda tough life, but you don't know *shit*." Tara ordered two tequila shots and told Spider that her first boyfriend had gotten her pregnant and given her gonorrhea at the same time.

"Whoa," Spider said. "That's one I haven't heard before." Crank sat down, flipping his blonde hair. He showed them the gram of cocaine he'd bought from some guy he'd met in the can. Tara's eyes lit up and she stopped talking about anything important.

The next morning after the breakfast piss stop two bikers passed the van, side by side. They wore identical jean vests over black leather and their long hair blew behind them in the wind. Spider waved and one saluted her as they passed. She was up in the passenger seat, feet on the dashboard. In the back Baldo and Crank rolled dice and drank JD. Tara snored delicately from the bunk. Spider had to roll a huge joint when Eddie put in Edith Piaf. He was one of the meanest looking guys she'd ever seen play punk rock and at that moment he was listening to a French chanteuse sing love songs. The moment was too surreal and she wanted to smoke and stretch it out even longer.

dirtbags > 217

Baldo was completely lovesick. They sat in the back together as Crank drove and Eddie slept, Tara fumbling at the radio in the front. Baldo confessed to Spider that he was the son of a famous Canadian poet. He tried to write poetry and everyone, including him, knew he would never be as good as his father. There was a kind of cavalier hopelessness to this Spider couldn't help but admire.

He told Spider how difficult it was for him to read his father's books, how he had learned his aunt was raped by rednecks, and of his mother's three loveless affairs. Baldo, unlike Crank, and maybe even Eddie, would fall in love at truck stops, with campground attendants, the blonde at an ice cream parlour. He rubbed Tara's shoulders and crooned. Tara drew a star across her belly with a black felt pen, a clear act of boredom.

"I want a real shower with shampoo," Tara moaned. There were two cherries on a stem tattooed on each of her shoulders. She looked at Crank and said, "A long, hot, steamy shower." Everyone agreed to chip in for a motel. When they got inside Tara immediately locked herself in the bathroom. Crank turned on a TV movie and passed out the rest of the six-pack. They were mesmerized by an android wiping out the population of L.A.

After awhile Tara came out in a towel and lied down beside Crank. There was a patch of grass down by the highway where Eddie and Spider decided to go sit with some beer. The night wasn't too cold and they listened to the occasional roar of a semi going past.

"Are you glad you came?" Eddie asked.

"Sure I am," Spider said. "I've never been anywhere. And I think I'm getting a lot of good shots."

"Is that all?"

"Of course not," she said.

By the time they got back to the room they were very drunk. So were Tara and Crank. They didn't seem to know what had happened to Baldo. Somehow Tara kept ending up on the bed, trying to wrestle Eddie. "Someone needs to get a sense of humour," she said, looking at Spider. Eddie took Spider's hand and they went outside to the van. Afterwards Spider wrote her name on the wood paneling in delicate black felt so someone, in the future, would know she'd been there.

In the morning, everything looked different.

Crank had a friend who lived on a farm in Oregon. They bought a bag of mushrooms and a half-ounce of weed then stopped at a park area on a river. Spider had not eaten mushrooms for a while and uneasily remembered her last few trips. She made sure she ate a little less than everyone else. They did shots of tequila from the bottle and gnawed orange slices to rinds. The spaces between their teeth were like black holes and beyond—the hum of the day grew louder and Spider felt Johnny smile down.

They perched on the bank of the river like great mud gods. A red bicycle was discarded in the weeds. Eddie talked about visiting Thailand. He wanted to see more of the world, but was scared of tsunamis and erupting volcanoes. "I used to think death by natural disaster was somehow pure," Spider said. "But I don't think that anymore." A well-dressed woman burst out from the trees. She looked at them with disdain then walked briskly down the path, clutching her handbag.

Eventually it grew cold. Everyone wanted pancakes so they drove until they found a restaurant. Spider felt her eyes become huge dark orbs that could absorb the tiniest details: the oil slick on a soupspoon, the fine cobweb lines between the fingers of the aging waitress. Spider saw death in the kitchen and flies in every room. Her breath was so hot she felt it melting her chin like wax. They got back in the van and she smoked a big joint to come down.

dirtbags > 219

Eddie curled up with her in the back. "The rats are running around in my brain," Spider said. He murmured stories in her ear until she finally fell asleep.

Spider's love for Eddie was like a rare and precious currency. She tried to control her dark fits of silence, bouts of sarcasm. As Eddie drove he told her stories: crazy ex-band mates, his father's dim-witted girlfriends, the beautiful women in the whorehouses of Spain. She admired how Eddie's tattoos moved on his forearm when he turned the wheel. "What was the last fight you were in?"

"Last year there was a brawl with skinheads in a parking lot," he said. "One of them jumped up onstage during the show, and I held out the microphone as if to pass it to him then hit his nose with it. A gang of them waited outside afterwards." Spider imagined his huge, meaty fists connecting to someone's face again and again. Eddie said he hated to fight, but when he got angry a white space in him took over. "You can't mess with my girl or my guitar," he said. "Or you will see a very different side of me."

In the back of the van the others carried on with their nonsense: "I'm smoking your last cigarette."

"Fuck you, shit-giblet!"

"Turd curd!"

"I'm a pirate."

"An ass pirate, maybe."

"Baby, I'm the pirate of love."

On a bench outside a rest area Spider saw carved in the old, scarred wood: "Dear Elizabeth, I'm waiting."

She had spent her life moving too fast to see such delicacies.

Spider took a black felt out of her purse and wrote her name on the bathroom wall of the pancake house. Someone had written a poem:
This is an aching world, disordered
smiling shards of children calculating worth
the absurdity of my existence
in this sour city stench.
She read it aloud to Tara who shrugged and kept rubbing lotion onto her feet. "So what's the deal with you and Eddie?'

"The deal is...I'm not sharing. What's up with you and Baldo?"

"Baldo? Just a sport fuck."

"Does *he* know that?"

A fat woman in a blue polyester pantsuit came into the bathroom and farted as she opened the stall door. They finished up and left.

There were in a poor neighbourhood trying to find directions when they pulled up to a man carrying a billboard that read, "Jesus saves, all others will burn." Spider reached for her camera and took a picture. The man had brown matted hair and orange teeth. "Pharisees and heathens," he sputtered when he looked in the window at Tara spread across the van floor, her and Baldo's tangled legs. Spider took another picture. Click. "I've had a near death experience," he said, "and now I know the true path." Click. Click. On a stoop across the street a young girl held a baby boy and watched them with dark eyes. Spider felt a sudden shame that she was taking pictures of a deranged and hungry man. But she didn't put her camera down.

There was a band the boys wanted to see, playing a packed bar in Arizona. For the first time Spider could really gauge how kids everywhere stayed the same.

She had an idea to put a photo collection together, of the little punk kids who stopped Eddie to talk to him. They were all jaded and sore like they'd seen it all before. Their philosophy was that true punks didn't get old but they liked Eddie, even though he was over thirty. The kids shuffled their feet while talking about being beaten by their parents or cops, abused by teachers or family friends. The stories had been repeated so often it didn't even make them flinch. Every time the teenage girls gave Spider a nervous smile it broke her heart. She knew it was a brutal, corrupt world for them to grow up in. At eighteen their scars had fully formed. It made Spider so hot with anger she burned all the way to her fingertips. She took their pictures to remember that.

A group of girls in the crowd linked arms, pushing up front together like a tidal wave. When one fell down the others pulled her back up. All night long the old men sang, while the kids danced with their demons beside them.

Eddie and Spider lay naked and sweaty in the motel bed. Spider had to fly home in a few hours. She'd already taken off extra days and had to be back at work, especially since she'd insisted on paying for half the plane ticket home. Eddie told her how much he was going to miss her when she left and said, "Spider, when I get back home we should get our own place."

"Where did that come from?" Spider rolled over and grabbed a cigarette from the pack on the nightstand.

"I've been thinking how it makes sense since when I'm in town I want to spend all my time with you and it always seems like you're struggling with rent."

"For the first time in my life I have my own place," she said. "No."

Eddie said, "I keep having this dream…"

"Do I want to hear this?"

"I'm driving a getaway car for these men in black turtlenecks. There's a girl in a blonde wig and white trench coat in the backseat with them. Alarms are going off, it's crazy. We take a few sharp turns but we're not gonna make it. Then I look in the rearview mirror and realize the woman in the blonde wig is you. You whisper in my ear, real soft, 'Eddie, watch the road.' And then we crash."

Spider sighed and closed her eyes.

"Let's find a house."

"A house?"

Eddie said, "Just think about it."

"It's too much dough for me right now," she said. She pushed her hair out of her face and looked at him. "We'd need a damage deposit, a phone, cable, electricity. And a house would mean I'd have to pay even more rent each month."

"Who cares about that? I'll take care of the difference. When you have money, all it does is make you realize you don't have to worry about it."

"No," she said, in a voice that meant drop it. "I can't depend on someone else like that ever again."

"We're in this together right?"

Spider nodded. "Yeah…"

"That's good," Eddie said. "Because I was lonely for the first half of my life and now I don't think I could go back to it."

"All right," Spider said. "I'll think about it." She burrowed under the covers, smiling. It didn't take much for Eddie to make her happy. When Spider woke up from a nightmare it calmed her just to hear him snore. She thought of how she'd spent hours, even days hiding out in her apartment from Eddie. He'd call and come to the window or knock on the door, and she'd stay in bed curled under the blanket, not breathing. She'd been too scared to love him. *Oh fuck,* she thought, *there's been so much wasted time.*

Eddie pulled her out from beneath the blankets and kept tickling until she got mad and threatened to start swinging. Then he stopped and lied across her, touching her face. She said, "I could set up a darkroom. Maybe I'll have two, but one will be my grow show."

Eddie said, "Whatever you want, babe."

She said, "Hell, we can have a garden and plant some fucking potatoes, too!"

Spider sparked the half-joint in the ashtray. They passed it back and forth and she told Eddie how in high school she used to raid gardens with her best friend Jenny White, hopping fences drunk and trampling everything in sight. She worried the same thing would happen to her garden. She said, "There would need to be some kind of security system. Three big mean dogs."

"Okay," he said. "But we'll need a little pussy to even it all out." She rubbed her small knuckles against his cheek.

"Oh yeah," she said.

Eddie Camaro was on top of the fucking world.

77

Spider stood in line at the CC Saloon. It had been awhile since she'd been there. The bar always stayed the same, which is why Spider loved the place and hated it, too. She always saw someone she knew. Blue and Sid were across the room.

Blue walked up and said, "Hey Hoochie." Spider had on a sheer, low-cut dress. They gave each other an awkward hug. "That dress is the perfect amount of class," Blue told her. "With just a touch of slut."

"Thanks," Spider laughed. "What's going on?"

"Not much. I heard you went on a road trip with Eddie. And *Tara* came too."

"Yeah, I got back a few weeks ago."

Blue invited Spider to join her and Sid. Spider got her drink and sat down. Blue told her she'd been visiting Angel and her sisters. One had started nursing school and another was dating a dwarf. "I haven't seen Angel in a long time." Spider said. "Am I still banned from her place?"

"Not sure."

"We had some crazy nights."

"I was there," Blue said. "I remember."

"I used to be a real mess back then," she said, and Blue didn't disagree. Spider wanted to smoke a joint and lie down. Her head hurt like she needed some sleep.

"Are you waiting for someone?" Blue asked.

"Not really." Spider pretended not to look around.

"What's going on?"

Spider snapped and said, "Nothing." Then she blurted, "Eddie wants us to get a house together."

"Why are you saying it like you've just found out you have cancer?"

"I'm not."

"I don't want to run you down but I think it's a bad idea." Blue looked so weary and scared it made Spider's guts churn.

"Well, all I know is I'm not going to move in with Eddie until I can pay my own way, out of principle." She knew she had stayed with Otis too long because she'd felt trapped and had nowhere to go. Sid interrupted and said he was going to order another pitcher. He stood for a moment and then Blue handed him a twenty-dollar bill. They watched him amble through the crowd.

"The problem is always money. When you're poor you don't have many fucking choices. But hooking up with another dirtbag isn't a very good one."

"Don't call Eddie a dirtbag!"

"I'm speaking metaphorically."

Spider looked at her suspiciously. "Hmmph."

"Look, it's not that I don't believe love exists for you and Eddie. All I'm saying is that even if two people get together and think it's a perfect match, it just won't last. Those feelings are a matter of circumstance. People say their bond gets stronger...*bullshit.* People settle. They get bored and cheat, they throw you back. Some can't handle it so they go crazy and murder or *kill* themselves over it. I say just take those first fucken moments and leave it alone. It's never going to get any better than that anyway."

"Sounds like you're talking about you and Sid, not me."

Sid came back just then with a pitcher of Guinness and Blue stopped talking. "He always goes for the good stuff," she said to Spider, "even though he never pays for it."

"Way to go, Sid."

"Thanks, Spider!"

Blue said to him, "Can you believe Spider and Eddie are getting their own fuck shack?" Sid mumbled something to the bottom of his glass.

Spider said, "I'm going to miss my apartment. Sometimes I smoke a joint and sit on the couch just admiring all the colours and art and how big my plants have gotten."

Two drunken blondes sat down at the end of their table. One girl said to her friend, "*How* can you like him? He's stupid like Mr. Potatohead."

Her friend said, "Yeah, but I'm still wringing out my panties from our last date!"

Spider and Blue looked at each other and broke up laughing like they hadn't done in a long time. Then a tall, rough-looking man in a denim vest tapped Spider on the shoulder. "I was waiting outside," he said. Blue stared him down.

"Hi Billy," Spider said. She looked at Blue. "This is Billy Newton. He was my prom date," she laughed. Blue did not look amused. Billy ignored her and sat down on the bench beside Spider, quietly spoke in her ear.

Billy touched Spider's arm. Spider didn't pull it away. She looked up and noticed Blue watching her, then in a louder voice asked Billy about Dave and the newborn twins. Then they stood up. "I'm going to walk Billy to his car," Spider said, avoiding Blue's eyes.

When Spider came back, Blue examined her from across the table. "What's going on with you, Spider?"

"These days the only thing I'm doing is getting high on developing fluid." Spider answered. "I was in the darkroom all day. Most of the pictures I tried to print didn't turn out, 'cause I'd forgotten to reset the shutter speed. The whole roll was under-exposed and it took me hours to salvage anything. I was

dirtbags > 227

so frustrated I kicked a wall and then got even madder because I hurt my foot doing it." Spider knew it would not be so easy to distract Blue.

"So, who was *that* guy?"

"I told you. He's from my hometown."

"He's got a dagger tattooed on his neck."

"What's the big deal if he does?"

"Are you cheating on Eddie with him?"

Spider looked down at her hands. "I wouldn't...call it *cheating*."

"So what is it? I know you're not as innocent as you seem. I watch you play people with those big brown eyes."

Spider frowned. "Okay look," she said. "I'm getting some bags of clip from him to make honey oil. He's going to buy it back from me and when Eddie gets home I'll have some money of my own so we can get a place together. That's my big plan. I'm an independent woman of the new order who does not rely on any man. Which reminds me...Sid, I totally need to borrow your van!"

When Spider stopped smiling she looked thoughtful and kind of sad. It was just how her face settled. She put on her coat and tied her hair back with a red scarf as Blue said goodbye. Spider smiled again, catching her own reflection in the window. It was surprising, for a moment, because Spider saw how she might become a beautiful woman, one day.

78

Spider drove out to Billy's to pick up the garbage bags of trim. He said he'd give her all the equipment, and a box of butane, too. She stood in his kitchen as he went through the process with her. She'd seen it done at Blue and Sally's once before.

Billy held up a cartridge made of plastic caps and PVC tubing. "It's called honey oil because of the colour. It's pure THC that's removed from the marijuana leaf. You load the shake into this then add a can of butane. Do it real slow," Billy stressed. "That rinses the THC crystals from the leaf. Then you squeeze the drops out into a hot pan. They freeze instantly. When they get re-heated the fumes cook off and what's left in the pan is oil. Scrape it into a test tube and cap it."

Spider knew that a few hits of honey oil from the end of a knife would leave her heavily stoned for hours. Whenever Sally Pepper and Spider could get their hands on some, which was rare, they loved to get ripped on it.

"What about the smell?"

"Just do it by a window with a fan. And you have to make sure the gas fumes can't reach any flames, like a pilot light. Don't forget and light a cigarette."

"What would happen?"

"It'll cause a flash fire and then..." Billy made an exploding sound with his mouth. He told her a story about the guy who'd blown his face off doing it with methyl-hydrate and died in the hospital with his lungs completely fried. The whole time Billy talked Spider could tell he enjoyed the attention. The only thing that mattered to her was how much money he would pay for each ounce. She figured she could make between six or seven hundred dollars in total, maybe more.

"Well, I'm going to go home and get started."

"Wait a minute," Billy said. He leaned back against the counter smiling. Spider stared back at him.

"Not this time," she said.

79

It took a few weeks for Spider to clean up the garbage bags of clip. Drying it out, getting rid of the leaves and stems, breaking up the shake. Staring at a row of skulls in the case of butane cans made Spider glad that Billy had gone through all the steps with her.

She phoned Sally one afternoon when the first batch of oil was ready. It was hard to hear over the fan in the background. "I can't wait for you to try this," Spider said. She felt like a little excited kid.

Her eyes were bloodshot when Sally arrived. "This took me a lot longer than I thought it would," she said. Spider pulled out a glass vial filled with gooey golden lumps. There was a row of them in a neat line along her kitchen counter. "Eddie's not supposed to be back for a couple more days. I'm so proud to finally have some useful skills to contribute to our relationship."

Sally said, "Whaddya mean? You're cute as hell and roll perfect joints!"

Spider buttered a paper and rolled it up with a bit of weed. It was a small joint black with oil. She said, "Are you ready to get high?"

Almost immediately Spider got really stoned, like there was a warm brick of air in the middle of her chest, spreading through her body. Her thoughts dripped off the walls and back into her head. The colours in the room mixed perfectly with each other, and the sounds of the street coming in the window, with Sally blowing out a cloud of smoke, her bright eyes smiling into Spider's.

"Oh Jesus," she said. "It's really good."

Sally and Spider gobbled ice cream in the kitchen hours later when the phone rang. Both were practically incapable of speech at that point and were instantly paralyzed with dread. Finally Spider answered it. It took her a minute to figure out it was Eddie. "I'm fine," she said. Her words came out very slow. "I'm with Sally Pipper. Nothing's wrooong."

When she hung up she told Sally, "Eddie called because he had a another bad dream about me. That's so overprotective and sweet." Spider did not tell Sally that Eddie had once said that if she died he'd last three days before he threw himself in front of a bus. Spider couldn't stop smiling about it.

"He's got a lot to lose," Sally said. "He loves you."

"Yeah, and most of the time I even believe the things he tells me!"

"Spider, look at you," Sally said. "You're beautiful and funny and smart and talented and sweet."

Spider took another hit. "Sally, all those hours we spent drinking, and waiting, the nights it rained, the hangovers, being hungry and having no money, I see it as the finest schooling, that I acquired the skills for the small triumphs of my life."

She was going to live with a man who loved her, and they were going to travel the world together. She didn't want to say it out loud because it scared her to feel so hopeful.

dirtbags > 231

80

The next night Billy Newton came to get the honey oil. Spider did not like having him in her apartment. He took up an uncomfortable space, and his eyes pried into things. It relieved her to know it was going to be one of the last times she saw him. She said, "I'm in the middle of a batch right now."

"How's it coming," he asked, nodding to the oil vials in a shoe box on the counter. Billy moved closer. She smelled whisky and cigarette smoke.

"I'm not quite done yet, but you can take most of it."

"You don't have to rush." As Billy moved closer the phone rang.

"Just a minute," she said. "Hello?" It was Eddie.

"Hey baby, I got home early."

"Heeey…you're back in town already?"

"I just got home from the airport and dropped off my gear. I'm in a cab on the way over. I'm gonna grab you and hu—"

"Okay. Gotta go. Bye."

Spider hung up and looked at Billy. She said, "That was my boyfriend. He just got back to town and he's on his way over. You can't be here."

Billy sat down heavily on one of Spider's kitchen chairs as she continued at the stove. "How long?"

"What?"

"The old man. How long?"

"I don't know, a while."

"You never told me about him."

She could never explain it to Billy so he'd understand. Spider loved Eddie because he kept everything important to him in his pockets, but was generous like a rich man and tasted like the sun.

He slept with his arm tucked around her tightly, almost scared she'd get away and he'd written a song about her brother called "Johnny Sunset" that made her cry. Spider washed the dishes and Eddie made them food and played music and Spider saw how it could be a good life. She told him, "We're different, but move easily together."

Billy stood up. His arms were stiff, jaw clenched. "What about me? I'm in love with you, Spider."

"No, you're not."

"I love you."

"That's crap."

"DON'T SAY THAT!" Billy roared until his face crumpled and he begged, "Spider please…"

Spider said nothing. She put on the oven mitts and took out another batch of drying weed. Then she put it on the counter and said, "Billy, after you pay me for this oil I'm never going to see you again. And you know it."

Billy took a stack of bills from his wallet and threw them at her. They fluttered prettily to the floor. "Fucking CUNT," he said. "This is all you ever wanted from me."

She said, "I'm sorry it turned out this way."

81

When Eddie got home from the airport it was late in the evening. He dropped off the gear in his apartment and kept the taxi waiting while he called to see if Spider was home. All day long nothing had moved fast enough for him.

The taxi stopped in front of Spider's place and Eddie looked up at her window. It was lit and for an instant he saw a man in her kitchen. Eddie got out of the cab and crept down the sidewalk. The bushes moved like shadows in the corner of the yard. Eddie crossed to the front door of the building. He buzzed Spider's apartment but she didn't answer and he tried again. When he looked back up at the window it was closed.

"He's here already," Spider said. Outside, Eddie called up to her window. "Billy, just get the fuck out!"

"Spider," Billy said. She turned to look at him. His voice was soft, and that made her afraid.

Eddie called up at Spider's apartment and buzzed her again. The explosion ripped through the night air, shattering the window in a rain of glass and fiery wood.

He saw the frame of Spider's kitchen window burning, then stared for a moment in confused shock at the river of blood down his arm. Eddie shouted, beat his fists and feet against the door and when it opened he pounded up the stairs to her apartment and flung his body into the smoke and fire. Then he saw Spider and couldn't stop screaming her name.

In a flash Spider was in the dream and it always went the same. She woke up in bed in a house she shared with Eddie. It was late morning and the sun came through the window, making everything bright and warm. Then she realized no one was beside her. But just before she called out she heard the creaking wooden porch and the front door opening, footsteps coming toward the bedroom. The sound echoed down the hallway.

The long night was over and she wasn't alone.

She'd almost been at the door when Billy lit his cigarette. That was the moment he had to keep.

82

Eddie quit the band. He started playing his own music and put out a few records that made him famous but it wasn't anything he wanted. When he came to town he always called and left tickets but Sally never went. She hoped he understood. It was too hard when everything came over her at once.

The light circling Eddie at the microphone stand looked like an angel coming down. His sad, lost eyes searched the crowd when he told them, "These are Spider songs."

Acknowledgments:

My thanks to Brian Kaufman and Anvil Press
for their patience and hard work;

To Carolyn Swayze, my agent, the best around;

To Chris Hutchinson and Billeh Nickerson for reading this
manuscript and the BC Arts Council for giving me a grant;

To my family of Mike, Terry, Heather, Rachel, Ashley,
Kathleen, Logan, Chuck, and especially my mother Sharon,
a kind, rare, generous, and strange woman;

To the ones who helped along the way: Todd Baiden, Alex
Cieslik, Ben Lightning, Jada Stark, Sandra Sanders, Amber
Stobey, Bronwyn Absalom, Anita Bruce, Sherry Berry Finn,
Katherine Scott, Toni Gallows, Sherry Brost, Nic Nolet,
Second-hand Rose, the Real McKenzies and Mark Boland...

And most of all, to the Fuckin' Little Bitches, everywhere!